STEVE BYE
611 - 10th St., N.W.
Austin, Minn.

FALCON  BOOKS

Patty and Jo, Detectives

BY ELSIE WRIGHT

The prospect of a dreary Christmas vacation at Miss Langton's School for Young Ladies is suddenly brightened for the Faraday twins, Patty and Jo, when they receive an invitation from their guardian, Welton Duer (whom they have never seen) to visit him. They arrive eagerly at Harker's Cove—only to discover that Duer has disappeared.

Undaunted by the efforts of the Japanese manservant to keep them from unraveling the mystery, these clever teen-agers become involved in all sorts of adventures. The Faraday twins embody the vivaciousness and self-assurance of all teen-age girls today—and their adventures will be your adventures.

Other FALCON BOOKS for Girls:

JEAN CRAIG GROWS UP

JEAN CRAIG IN NEW YORK

JEAN CRAIG FINDS ROMANCE

JEAN CRAIG, NURSE

CHAMPION'S CHOICE

The door opened behind Patty and Jo.

Patty and Jo

DETECTIVES

by

ELSIE WRIGHT

THE WORLD PUBLISHING COMPANY

CLEVELAND AND NEW YORK

Falcon Books

are published by THE WORLD PUBLISHING COMPANY

2231 West 110th Street · Cleveland 2 · Ohio

Contents

Contents

PATTY AND JO, DETECTIVES

CHAPTER 1

Introducing Patty and Jo

PAT FARADAY sat gazing disconsolately out of the window of her room in Miss Langton's School For Young Ladies, at what the catalogue of that select institution described as its "spacious, wooded grounds." At the moment, the grounds were spacious and wooded, but hardly impressive, nor was Pat, who had viewed them from this window more or less constantly for six years, in a mood to be impressed.

December had done things to the landscape, stripped the trees of their leaves, turned the flower beds to straggly wisps of crackling stalks, and left the still unfrozen pond a murky, muddy gray. The late afternoon sun, setting in a misty haze, shone through the skeletons of the black trees, adding not brightness, but a further gloom to the scene.

The gloom fitted Pat's mood. She was pondering the strange ways of Fate, and those ways were not to her liking. More specifically, she was wondering about

measles. Not that Pat had measles herself—no, indeed.
June Martin had measles, and while June Martin, aged
six, was in no way related to Pat Faraday, her measles
were about to spoil Pat's Christmas vacation. You see,
Pat had been invited to spend her vacation from Miss
Langton's School For Young Ladies with the Martin's,
the family of her classmate, Peg. But June, otherwise
quite a nice child, had suddenly developed a general un-
easiness and assorted pink spots that were nothing less
than the measles with which we are so concerned.

Another boring Christmas spent at school, with only
the acid Miss Langton, and the genial but stupid Miss
Fraser! At the thought Pat slumped still lower, if possible, into her chair. Of course, there'd be Jo, too. A ray
of light broke through the thick gloom. Jo always made
life more livable. Pat got up and went to the window,
pressing her nose against the cold surface, in order to
see if by chance Jo had come back from her walk,
and was approaching the dormitory.

Jo Faraday was the other half of the Faraday twins.
The practical half, the half that stayed down on the
ground while the other half soared in the clouds. "The
stodgy half," said Jo. "The better half," said Pat. But
we can't take for evidence these personal descriptions
of either of them, because they are, of course, preju-
diced. But whichever half was which, neither could have
existed without the other. Only together did they make
up a whole. It is true that Patty was imaginative, ro-

mantic, and given to dramatizing her life; Jo was practical and prosaic. But good sport that she was, she would follow the temperamental Patty's wanderings like a faithful puppy, not understanding quite, but adoring nevertheless. And when danger threatened, or the flights went too far afield, there she was to drag them both back to safety.

In appearance they were almost identical. Sixteen years old—both of them. Tall and slender, both of them, just grown out of the gawky thinness of the awkward age into the litheness of young girlhood. Brunette, both of them, with brown curls that clustered in unruly mops all over their round heads, and brown eyes that gleamed with impish fires that would not be quenched, even when the occasion called imperatively for demureness. In short, the Faraday twins were pretty.

Their identity of appearance, coupled with the imagination of Pat, and the ability of both of them to get themselves into situations, had made life interesting, if nothing else, to the teachers of Miss Langton's, from the very day, six years ago, that they had come there. Of course, they did those things that all twins find delight in doing. They went to class for each other— they answered questions for each other when one of them was in a tight place. But gradually each teacher worked out the problem in her own way—usually by seating them on opposite sides of the room, so that the only way they could answer for each other was by ventriloquism, which neither could ever quite master, although they spent many hours in the attempt. Now only Miss Fraser, gentle and absent-minded, still called Pat "Jo," and Jo "Pat."

Pat shuddered when she thought once more of spending two weeks with the mild Miss Fraser. And why did the campus have to look so dismal now? She never noticed it at other times. After all, when you've spent six years at a place, the surroundings become so much a part of you that you never do notice them. Except at a time like this, when you wanted so much to get away from them. Jo wasn't in sight. The view out the window was one of ghastly emptiness. Pat walked listlessly over to the daybed and threw herself down on the flowered spread. She wished that she had some of Jo's temperament. Here was the girl out for a walk, enjoying herself in animal exercise, when she had just received the same blow that had laid Pat so low. How could the feelingless Jo go rambling off when she knew that she was doomed to spend another deadly vacation at school? Jo never brooded on Fate.

Pat, aided and abetted by her comfortable position upon the bed gradually began to brood a little less on Fate, and let her mind play on more pleasant subjects. Suppose she and Jo weren't orphans. They'd have a home to go to. June Martin could have all the measles in the world, and they wouldn't care. Oh, of course they'd care, but it wouldn't have spoiled their vacation the way it had. Well, they'd be going home. She got that far. But even with her active imagination, Pat found it hard to go further. What sort of home would they be going to? As a matter of fact, the Faraday twins had never known a real home.

Their mother died when they were born. Pat had seen pictures of her, and she knew what she would look like, when she greeted them, her twins, home for the holidays. She would be young, and laughing-eyed and pert, and she would be very glad to see them, and laugh with them when they told her their adventures at Miss Langton's. At first she might pretend to be stern, but she would have to smile a little, and then break out in a little giggle, and they'd all laugh together. You could tell that that's what she'd be like, just from her picture. And she would have their room all ready for them with all the lovely things that girls like—with silk pillows that she had made for them herself, and funny little gingham dogs, and floppy dolls. And of course, ruffled curtains. Pat looked at the straight, severe draperies that hung at the windows of their room, and were an exact duplicate of the draperies that hung at the windows of every room at Miss Langton's School. "Simplicity," said Miss Langston, "and practicability are the keywords of our furnishings here." Too true, thought Pat. But dear me, couldn't someone put in the word "beauty" someplace? Pat thought that it would make a very nice keyword. Their mother would have had that for her keyword, she knew. So of course, there'd be lovely crisp curtains with little ruffles that stuck out perkily all around their edges.

She couldn't remember any ruffled curtains at Aunt Harriett's. Pat shuddered a little when she thought of Aunt Harriett's. Everything there she remembered as being heavy and thick and red—the draperies, the rugs, the hangings that covered the plaster walls. Aunt Harriett's was the first place the twins had lived. Not that you could call it their first home—it wasn't a home at all. Aunt Harriett, who was really their great-aunt, never smiled at all. She believed that children should be seen and not heard, and if possible, not even seen. She hadn't approved of her niece's marriage to Martin Faraday, the young engineer, and she didn't approve of the twins. But she felt it her duty to take them and take them she did, into the cold, barren atmosphere of her forbidding home. Once there, she turned them over to a succession of nurses and governesses of assorted temperaments and degrees of kindness.

Pat remembered most of them vividly. They ranged from Nana, who left them to work out their own salvation while she read lurid stories in the Sunday supplements, to Miss Martha, who slapped them when they broke any of the tyrannical rules that she set up for them. There were many in between, but not one of them, so far as Pat could remember, did anything to relieve the chill monotony of their drab existence. They were lovable children, but Aunt Harriett seemed to have a genius for picking out women as cheerless and cold as herself to look after them. She gave them food and shelter and care. Their clothes were clean and mended. What more did a child need? The answer is easy. They were starved for love.

The only rays of light in those years were the hurried visits of their father, who stole time off from the building of bridges to see his daughters. He would come breezily into the room and swoop them up in the air. Pat remembered that he smelled like outdoors and tobacco, and had his pockets crammed with good things to eat that horrified Aunt Harriett and their current governess; and his suitcase was full of amusing toys that those worthy ladies declared not at all suitable for children, but which were great fun and very exciting. The visits were all too short. They were so gay and jolly that Pat and Jo forgot all the dull days that had gone before, and never thought to tell this wonderful man about Nana and Beatrice and Martha and all the other horrible women who were supposed to be taking care of them so well. But when they were over, how much duller their lives seemed by contrast!

There was one compensation for those days. As soon as they were able to read, the twins lost themselves in books. They read everything that they could find, and especially the books that their father left for them, or sent to them from faraway places. And even in those days each twin had developed her own taste, so that Pat was reading fairy tales and the *Arabian Nights*, and imagining herself the heroine of many fanciful adventures, Jo preferred such books as *Five Hundred Things for a Boy To Do*. Although she was not permitted to do one-five-hundredth of the fascinating things set forth, it delighted her practical soul to read the lovely descriptions on how to build a bird house, and to imagine just what she would do with a hammer and some boards.

When they were eight, a wonderful thing happened. Their father took them away from Aunt Harriett's. He had arrived unexpectedly one day and found them in tears. They had told him, then, about how lonesome they were, both of them talking at once. They told him of the endless days shut up in the grim old house, with no friends to play with, and no one to love them, and only Martha, who was cruel to them, to see that they were taken care of at all. Their father had left them rather abruptly. On his face was a look that they had never seen before, and saw only once afterwards, when he was dismissing a contractor who had been found using defective materials in his work. In a little while he came back.

"I'm taking you away from here, my dears," he had said. They hadn't understood him at first. He looked at their bewildered faces for a long moment and said

eaten on the bank of a stream, just at sunset, and how bland were the wholesome pot roasts of Susan, the cook, after tortillas, tamales and other spicy foods of South America.

But there was always the gleaming hope, underneath all this imprisonment, that it was only for a year, and that in a few months they would be free again, to hit the trail with their dad. Then came the news of his sickness, and on the heels of that, word of his death. Pat didn't like to think of that time. It was the blackest moment of their lives. Pat shook her head a little and buried it in the pillow to blot out the memory.

They had been provided for by a trust fund. Welton Duer had been appointed executor of his friend's estate, to look after the twins. Welton Duer. Pat said the name over to herself, to hear the sound of it. She liked it.

Welton Duer was the big mystery of the twins' life. They had never seen him. He had been their father's best friend. At Aunt Harriett's they had never even heard his name mentioned. Aunt Harriett had not approved of him. Aunt Harriet had not approved of a great many persons, and a great many things. For example, archaeology. Archaeology was Welton Duer's profession. According to Aunt Harriett, a person should let well enough alone. Why couldn't that crazy friend of Faraday's get some occupation, and not go gallivantin' about digging up old bones? Who wanted the

bones, anyway? Who wanted to know how those old
heathens lived, setting up their odd images to worship
instead of God. No good would ever come of it, she
knew. And she wasn't going to talk to the twins about
him, either. What they didn't know wouldn't bother
them, and they were full enough of fancy ideas without
giving them any more. Why did those poor children
have to take after their father, she wondered. That was
Aunt Harriett.

Their father hadn't said much more about Welton
Duer. The twins understood that at one time the two
men had been inseparable, but after they once became
established in their professions, the one's engineering
jobs, the other's expeditions, had kept them apart.
When he was made their father's executor, and their
guardian, he had been in the United States long enough
to make provisions that the twins should stay on at
Miss Langton's until they were graduated. He provided
them with money for their expenses, and made arrangements that they should receive a regular allowance, just as they had when their father was alive.
After that, he had dealt only with Miss Langton, writing to her when he had any message to convey to Pat
and Jo, which he rarely did. He never wrote to his
wards, never came to see them. It was as though they
did not exist for him.

But he existed for the twins. They talked about him
often, and had some very definite ideas about the sort

of man he was. The opinions were mostly unfavorable. How lovely, thought Pat now, if Welton Duer were not a gruff old bear who didn't like them at all, and was rather annoyed at having to be responsible for them. Right now he might send them an invitation to spend Christmas with him at some romantic place—say—well, Yucatan.

Pat settled back more comfortably on her pillow and let her mind dwell lovingly on Christmas in Yucatan. They would be exploring some old Mayan ruins, of course. And there would be Pat, dressed in breeches and a sun hat, leading an expedition into a newly discovered old temple. The great stone door, for long centuries unopened, would be rolled back, revealing a long flight of stairs. Down this stairway, long undefiled by human feet, she would majestically walk. The others might hang back a little—who knew what fate awaited them below? But she walked bravely on, ahead of them all. At the bottom was another door. Slowly she pushed it back. Within was a room of untold splendor. Its walls were of gold, set with turquoises and other precious stones. The floor was of stone. And all about the glittering room were chests. Pat approached one of the chests. She pulled at the top. At first it resisted her efforts to open it, but then its lock gave way and the top flew up. It was filled with precious jewels that shone like stars.

Pat was about to dip her hands into the treasure

when she felt a pressure on her shoulder. She turned about and beheld a strange apparition. Something was standing behind her, something that had the body of a woman and the head of a strange bird with a long beaked nose. This strange creature shook Pat by the shoulder and opened her mouth to speak.

But the words that issued forth were no strange chant or rune of ancient days. They were common, everyday English words.

"Hi, Pat, wake up!"

Pat sat up and shook her head. Jo was standing above her, shaking her by the shoulder and calling to her. When she was fully awakened, she stammered, "What do you mean, wake up? I wasn't sleeping!"

"You weren't sleeping? You certainly were! You were sound asleep!"

"I was not!" said Pat indignantly, and yawned. "Where on earth have you been?"

"Oh, I went down to the pond to see if it was frozen, and it wasn't, and I got my feet wet, and I went to the woods to see if there were any nuts left, by any chance, and there were, but they were all wormy, and I walked down to the village to see if there was anything exciting to do or see, and there was." Jo took a long breath.

"What was exciting in the village?" asked Pat hopelessly, because there was never anything exciting in the village.

Jo looked mysterious, but because she was a very

frank person and could not keep a secret longer than two seconds at the most, she blurted out, "We got a letter. I stopped at the postoffice to see if there was any mail for the school, and there was a letter for us."

"A letter?" Pat was all ears. "From whom?"

"From Welton Duer," said Jo.

"Oh, for heaven's sakes, let me see it," Pat almost shouted. "Is it from Yucatan?"

"Yucatan?" asked the practical Jo. "Why, no. It's postmarked Harker's Cove, Michigan. I wonder how he got up there."

"Probably lives there, Jo-Jo. Why don't you open the letter? What do you suppose he has to say?" Pat was beside herself with curiosity and wonder. She'd just been thinking of her guardian—and now a letter from him—"For goodness sakes, open it, darling."

Jo laughed. "All right, I'm opening it." She tore open the envelope, which was white, plain and unrevealing, and spread out the long single sheet of heavy white parchment paper, covered with a bold, black handwriting. It wasn't a very long letter, but the large scrawl took up the whole sheet. With their heads together, the two girls read the first words that Welton Duer had ever written to them.

"My dear Josephine and Patricia," it began formally, and then plunged directly into the matter at hand, as though he had been in the habit of writing these letters to them every fortnight, instead of every decade. "I should be very pleased to have you spend your Christmas vacation with me at Harker's Cove. Miss Langton informs me that this vacation starts almost immediately, and that she is willing to have you make this trip, if you so desire. She will make the necessary arrangements to get you here safely, and if you will wire me the time of your arrival, I shall see that there is someone to meet you at the station."

Pat looked at Jo and Jo looked at Pat. "Oh, my," said Jo. "What a cordial invitation!"

"But an invitation, nevertheless," said Pat, wide-eyed. "Oh, Jo, why do you suppose he sent it at all?"

"Maybe because he wants us to visit him. After all, he must have heard what charming young ladies we are. You don't suppose that they haven't heard about us even at Harker's—what's the place—" Jo consulted the letter—"at Harker's Cove. Why, our fame must have spread the length and breadth of the country."

"Don't be silly, Jo. Not any sillier than you can help being. Really—why do you suppose the old bear has suddenly come out of his den and asked us to visit him?"

Jo was being obstreperous. She shared her sister's curiosity at the strange invitation, but it suited her to express herself in teasing, rather than in conjecturing as to the why and wherefore of their strange guardian's request. "He hasn't come out of his den. You aren't consistent, sister. He has asked us into his den."

Pat was scanning the letter again, as though it would give her some clue to the purpose behind it. "But why?" she persisted. "Jo, there's something behind this. We must find out. We must be wary."

Jo thought so, too, but she wouldn't admit it. "Maybe he's asked us because he wants us, that's all. He's suddenly got sociable, and wants company. And who would be better company than us, if I must say so, as shouldn't."

"But he's an archaeologist," went on Pat, significantly.

Jo pretended that she understood this last strange statement, and then had to admit that she didn't. "What has that to do with it?" she asked.

"Just this. Archaeologists don't just suddenly become sociable. They are strange men. They dabble in mysteries. They are versed in strange doings."

Jo listened in amazement. "Why, you've never seen an archaeologist!"

Pat withered her with a glance. "There are some things, my child, that one just *knows*. Mark my words. There will be strange doings at Harker's Cove."

"I hope there's good skating," was all Jo said to this amazing news. "Where is Harker's Cove, anyway. Where's that atlas?" She dashed over to Pat's desk, and rummaged in the jumbled heap of books and papers that covered it. "Why can't you be orderly? I'm sure

you borrowed my atlas just yesterday. What did you
do with it?"

Pat waved vaguely with her hand. "Oh, it's somewhere about. You'll find it."

Jo did find it, and hastily turned from the index to
the map of Michigan. "It's not here," she said. "Harper,
but not Harker's Cove. Well, anyway," tossing aside
the book, "a 'cove' sounds like good skating. We'll take
along our skates. And our skis." She dashed over to
their wardrobe closet. "We'll take our new red sweaters
that we got to wear down to the Martin's." She bur-
rowed her way busily in among the dresses and coats.

Pat, who had thrown herself back among the pillows,
stretched luxuriously, little concerned with the practical
details of what she would wear on the scene of what
she knew would be strange happenings. "I wonder what
he looks like," she said.

"Who?" asked Jo.

"Welton Duer."

"Oh, he's ancient." Jo's voice was muffled. Then it
became clear as she flew out into the room again with
an armful of woolly things. "He's probably forty years
old. He has a long white beard."

"Oh, no, not a long white beard!"

"Oh, yes," insisted Jo. "He's an archaeologist. They
all have long white beards."

"You never saw an archaeologist!"

Jo wrinkled up her nose and grinned at her sister,

who had walked so unwittingly into her own trap. "There are some things," she laughed, "that one just *knows!*"

Pat had to laugh too, then she became sober again. "He has deep eyes. Suffering eyes. He has looked upon strange things."

"I wonder if he'll like our skiing outfits."

Pat did not deign to answer. Her eyes looked far away. "Jo," she said finally, "we are going to a strange adventure at Harker's Cove. I feel it. A man does not break a silence of so long for nothing. There is some purpose in Welton Duer's invitation. There is some mystery here, and it is a mystery millions of years old. A man who has tampered with the idols of the Mayans is never again a free man. He is a marked man."

A sudden gong rang through the house.

"Dinner," said Jo. "We'll ask Miss Langton about tickets and things after dinner. Thank heavens we're not staying here for our vacation."

"We may be glad to come back to this place," said Pat ominously.

"Maybe," said Jo. "But Harker's Cove will have to be pretty bad to make me long for Miss Langton's. Here, you hurry up and get washed. The second gong is going to ring."

Slave to long habit, Pat jumped off the bed, grabbed up a comb from her dressing table, and began a hasty toilet before going down to dinner.

CHAPTER 2

Dead or Alive

MISS LANGTON got them to Harker's Cove all right, and there they were. Snow had followed them during the long train trip, and now it lay all about them as they stood on the empty platform of the tiny railroad station. Snow and nothing else. Unless you counted the wind that whistled about them and playfully ran up their congealing spines. Pat and Jo huddled together for warmth and surveyed the snowy scene.

The station was set at the edge of a dark pine forest that rose behind them. "Mysterious," said Pat, and shuddered with cold and mystery.

"If it's mysterious, it certainly hides the mystery of the person who was supposed to meet us here. I'm freezing. Let's go inside."

This brilliant suggestion, which certainly should have been made sooner, met with immediate approval, and the girls made for the door. But just as they got there it opened, and the stationmaster, who had taken his time looking them over from his warm post inside, came out.

He surveyed them carefully as they clung together, shivering.

"You the gels Mr. Duer's expecting?" he asked, as though trains stopped at the Cove every day letting off two pretty girls dressed exactly alike.

"We are," said Jo with as much dignity as she could muster, considering her chattering teeth. "Is there someone to meet us?"

The stationmaster pulled his cap and thought about this. Then he recalled, "Wal, yes, there's someone comin' to meet ya, but you'd both better come in and wait. It may be sometime yet before he gets here."

Without another word, he turned and went back into the station, leaving the twins to follow. It was deliciously warm in there. A fat, pot-bellied stove gave forth a good heat, and Pat and Jo, ignoring the surly stationmaster, went over to it and warmed themselves at its genial front. The stationmaster, ignoring them, went through a door, and reappeared at the little wicket behind which he pretended to be engrossed in his business. The wicket really acted as a screen, where he took up his real business of watching the twins.

At first the two did not notice this scrutiny, being intent upon getting warm. But soon, with the instinct that we all possess, they knew that they were being watched. Jo spoke first, turning her back so that the stationmaster could not hear what she said and lowering her voice. "He doesn't like us," she said.

"Evidently not. Or else he thinks that we are planning to steal something!" Pat giggled as she looked about the barren room, with its hard wooden benches running around two sides, and the tattered signs announcing summer excursion rates on the plaster walls. "I'd really like some of the signs for curiosities," she added, "but I hardly think they're very valuable in themselves."

"Those benches are real antiques. The carvings alone are worth their weight in gold." Jo indicated the whittled decorations and intertwined initials that covered the hard bench. Do you think that we dare sit on them?" She went over and sat gingerly down. The bench was as hard as it looked. Pat came over and sat down beside her. Here they were as far away as possible from the peering eyes of their new enemy, and could see out of the window to a road that wound away from the station, and seemed to skirt the forest, or enter it—they could not tell which at this distance.

"There's something funny about this," said Pat. "I feel that there's something sinister in the air."

Jo sniffed. "That's just bad ventilation," she said irreverently.

"You're incorrigible," Pat said, hurt at the lack of sympathy in her too prosaic sister. She forgot her hurt, however, in a deeper concern. She leaned closer toward her sister. "Why do you suppose that he's so suspicious of us?"

Jo, who would not admit that she was worried, tried to appear as unconcerned as possible. But to herself she had to admit that her own courage was ebbing. "He's probably just naturally of a suspicious nature," she said lightly. She could see no reason for his actions, though. The warm air, the ugly station room, the feeling of being deserted and stranded with this surly man began to oppress her.

"It's cold," protested Pat.

She went up to inspect a lurid poster on the wall. "Wanted, dead or alive."

"Ugh, what a hideous creature," she said. "I should hate to meet him here."

"Or anyplace, for that matter," said her sister.

"I'd like to meet somebody, though. Even if he looked like this. Oh, 'escaped convict. Believed to be hiding in the woods.' Oh, Jo, we're lost, let's get out."

"Anything's better than this. I'd rather freeze than stay here another minute." Jo jumped up hastily and went out to the platform, where she began to pace up and down. Pat followed her.

"I think we're deserted," she said.

"Nonsense," said Jo in her best manner. But a gale of wind blowing treacherously at her before the word was out of her mouth, shoved the vowels back down her throat, and made her swallow them, so that it sounded less reassuring than she had intended it to. "We can always go back to Miss Langton's."

Pat looked dubious. "There's probably no train out of this place for days," she said. "There's a schedule." She hurried over to read the chalked message on the blackboard. It was no message of hope. "We're here to stay," she said, with a shake of her head. "There's no train before day after tomorrow. They seem to run only every other day. We're trapped. Let's get in out of the cold, anyway. If anybody is coming for us, and I don't think anybody is, he may as well find two living girls and not frozen corpses." Pat suited her actions to her words, and opened the door into the waiting room. But just as she was about to go in, a strange noise reached their ears from the direction of the woods. It was something like the sound of a tank crossing enemy territory, protected by a barrage of machine guns. Pat and Jo looked at each other, and then, with one accord, rushed around to the back of the station.

Coming down the road was their Lochinvar, not on a shining steed, but in a noisy, rickety Ford, evidently the only machine that could bump over the icy ruts of that road without falling apart.

"Saved!" cried Jo.

"Saved!" squealed Pat, and they danced a dance in the snow. It was as though the marines were coming at the crucial moment, and they felt like the heroines of a drama that was almost a tragedy. Already it began to feel warmer. The wind was blowing less bitterly, and

the snow, instead of being menacing, and looking like a
blanket to cover them when they perished, like Babes
in the Woods, now formed a beautiful covering for the
rosy world. They could even have gone in and embraced
their enemy the stationmaster, but they preferred to
wait outside, to be ready for Welton Duer when he got
there.

They ran around to the platform, and began to collect
their odd assortment of luggage. Jo had taken the skis,
as promised, and they did make rather awkward handling, along with the rest of the lumpy bundles that lay
on top of their ordinary bags. Jo had just succeeded
in tangling herself up completely in the skis and an
Indian blanket, when the ancient Ford, with an angry
snort and a backfire, stopped beside the platform. The
door opened, and Lochinvar stepped out.

At first Jo wanted to laugh. He did look so funny.
But the expression on Pat's face, when she took a quick
surreptitious glance at her, forbade that. Pat's face expressed frozen unbelief. Of course, it was rather un-
believable, at first. Who would have expected that out
of the snowy wastes of Michigan would step a little
Japanese with a long black overcoat, derby hat, and ear
muffs to keep his oriental ears warm? That is exactly
what happened, however.

The strange figure approached them, grinning
broadly. Whether it was a grin of welcome or not, the

girls could not tell, since the expression never changed but constantly spread itself out in that intense smile, like a mask of comedy.

"Mlissee Josephine? Mlissee Platlicia?"

Jo, the first to recover her composure, nodded acknowledgment of these strange names.

"Me Yamoto. Take you Mlistee Dluer."

There seemed to be no answer to that. Nimbly he piled their luggage into the back seat, and since it took up all the room back there, Pat and Joe saw nothing else to do but ride up in front of that ancient car with Yamoto. Gallantly he held the door open for them, as though he, in full livery, were handing them into a limousine on Park Avenue, and then, still grinning, he got into the driver's seat and stepped on the starter. Jo saw the stationmaster quietly opening the door and staring at them, one last, long stare.

The car wouldn't start at first. It gave a few coughs and died. But Yamoto did not despair. He knew this car. Grinning pleasantly, he stepped on the starter again, pulled the choke in and out, jiggled the spark, and was rewarded by a hoarse rumble that indicated that the machine was of a mind to start. With a lurch they were on their way, heading straight into the black woods with only Yamoto for guide, and with no guarantee that the bouncing, skidding car would ever bring them back. Yamoto did not have much to say. In fact, he had nothing to say. Whenever his attention was not taken up wholly with the mechanics of driving over that perilous road, he turned on them his bland, toothy grin. Their only answer to this was a sort of wan smile, mustered up by a mighty effort.

When they had gone for a considerable distance, and it seemed that the car was not going to tip over with them and their luggage, Pat and Jo began to enjoy their ride. After all, it was an experience, to be driven into the Michigan woods by a Japanese named Yamoto, who wore a black coat with a velvet collar. How on earth did he get anything like that up here? Did he bring it with him from wherever he had come? He must have. Certainly he couldn't have bought that in the store in which the stationmaster had bought his sturdy mackintosh and felt cap. This outfit was a product of the extreme east.

The ride satisfied Pat's desire for the romantic, and Jo's for the sporting, for through the windows she could see that the woods were going to offer endless opportunities for snow sports. She was glad that she had brought her skis.

Yamoto broke in on their thoughts, rather unexpectedly. "Mlister Dluer not home," he said, and then went on hurriedly, as though reciting a piece after long rehearsal, "he called suddenly away. Implortant blusiness. No can stay. No be back for two weeks." He smiled at them.

Their faces were blank. Then Jo said, "But he—invited us—he told us—"

Yamoto could not account for the vagaries of occidental employers. He shrugged his shoulders, made unusually wide by the padding of his overcoat. Pat looked at Jo and Jo looked at Pat. Miss Langton would not have approved of this. In fact, they did not know whether they approved of it themselves.

Pat asked the question. "Who else is at Mr. Duer's Lodge? Has he any other—servants?"

Yamoto grinned. If he would only change his expression! Did he have to grin like that? Evidently he had to. It seemed to be a nervous habit. "Oh, yes, Mlissee. Mliss Gluba, she there. She always there. Keep house. Keep house for Mlister Dluer long time. Old lady." In this way did the twins find out that Miss Gluba would chaperon them on their strange vacation up north. Of course, "Gluba" didn't sound like much of anything, but anything would have been reassuring at this moment.

"When did Mr. Duer find that he had to go? Didn't he have time to let us know? He could have wired us up to yesterday not to come." Jo said.

"He find out lestiday that he have to go. He left lestiday. Big hurry."

"He left by train?" Pat asked quickly.

Yamoto stopped smiling for half a second, then answered blandly, "He left lestiday. Yamoto dlive him to stations."

Pat was silent then. She looked at Jo, who was regarding her curiously. But she couldn't talk then. All their conversation had to be carried on very loudly in order to be heard at all—above the clattering of the automobile. She had something to talk over with Jo though, as soon as they were alone.

"Is Mr. Duer often called away like this?" asked Jo of Yamoto, and realized that she was talking just to make conversation. "I suppose that somebody discovered a new ruin, and had to see him right away."

Yamoto evidently did not understand the trend of this conversation, but he smiled nevertheless. "He no go away vel' much. He stay home all time. Just had to go now." A particularly vicious stretch of road shut off all further talk. They were not headed into the woods, but were skirting it now. They could smell the sharp, icy tang of the pine trees, iced before it came to their nostrils, so that it went to their heads, and made them just a little intoxicated. Then the air grew spicier still, and tangier.

"The lake?" asked Jo.

Yamoto nodded. They came to the end of the woods and turned right, and there was the lake, about a mile ahead of them, in an angry gray line that was hardly distinguishable from the sky. It was about four o'clock now, and the sun was on its downward path, about to slip into the gray of the water like a ball of metal. The twins were entranced by the view and almost overlooked the fact that they were passing through a village.

" 'Arker's Cove," said Yamoto.

So this was Harker's Cove. No wonder it did not appear on the map. The village consisted of one street, the road on which they were driving, with small white houses on either side. All of them had signs "Tourists," or "Rooms." Some were dignified with names like "Bonnie View," and "Eclat." The two most pretentious buildings were large white wooden hotels, which now looked desolate and deserted. There was a Post Office, some chain stores with brightly colored fronts that had penetrated even into these fastnesses, and a general store which obviously had sold the stationmaster his mackintosh and his felt cap, for there were the counterparts in its windows.

It did not take long to pass through the village, that straggled down to the cliff that rose out of the lake. They were going at a pretty fast clip, taking advantage of a stretch of good road, and for a second Pat and Jo thought that Yamoto was going to drive them over the cliff and on to the frozen surface of the lake below, still smiling pleasantly. But the man evidently had other plans for their destruction, because he turned off to the right onto a road that led along the cliff.

"Pletty soon home," he reassured them.

The twins were not sorry. The wind off the lake had risen almost to gale proportions. Their feet and hands were nearly frozen; their faces tingled and ached. Yamoto, in his queer, unsuitable outfit, seemed cozy and, if not exactly warm, not uncomfortable. The sun was rapidly sinking, and on their right the woods looked darker than ever. There was a sudden flip of white in the darkness and a crashing sound.

"Dleer," said Yamoto.

Pat and Jo, although they had seen nothing, were thrilled. They had left civilization such a short distance behind, and were in the wilderness. But cold as they were, they wished that they had just a little civilization before them now, that is, enough to warm their hands and feet.

"Much further?" asked Jo hopefully.

"Here," said Yamoto succinctly. "Home." They entered an opening in the woods that was hardly perceptible from the road, and drove up a hard-packed driveway to the Lodge. It was all that Pat, in her imaginings, could imagine a Lodge to be. It was of logs, low and squat, with a wide porch running across the front. The rough slanted roof contained two gables, the only indication that it was a two-storied building. There were lights in the windows, and through the wide bay window the twins could see a fire burning. The forest as all around them; branches of pine brushed against them as they got out of the car, and walked with numb, stiff feet up the broad snow-swept steps to the rough-hewn door. Yamoto opened the door for them waving them in with a flourish; gratefully they preceded him into the lodge.

Their first impression was of warmth. At last it was deliciously, beautifully warm. Their second delight was the room itself. It was large—larger than the exterior of the house had seemed to promise. Its walls were of rough logs, but there were so many soft, luxurious chairs and couches about, and such thick, woolly rugs on the floor, that it gave no impression of primitiveness. The only hint of the primitive, they discovered, when they had a chance to look around (that is, when Yamoto went grinning out of the room to find the housekeeper), were the decorations. On all of the tables and shelves, on the top of the bookcase, in fact, on every available flat surface were odd Indian bowls and vases, clay idols of every sort, and carved wooden totem animals.

The twins stood in silence for a minute, in the midst of their luggage. They were absorbing impressions of the room, and absorbing the fragrant warmth given off by pine logs. Then Pat put her hand down casually on a small table standing next to her. It struck something hard. She looked down, and jerked her hand away as though she had been burned.

"Jo," she gasped.

Jo turned to her, amazed at the horror in her tone. "What's the matter?"

Pat could only point to the object on the table that she had touched. "Look!"

Jo looked. Her unemotional face, blown to a rosy hue by the wind, changed expression just a little, and became a shade less red. On the table, staring up at them, was a mummified head, tiny but extremely life-like. It had probably once been the prized possession of some long-dead jungle head hunter. Now, in the calm of a Michigan lodge, it changed the whole aspect of the room for a pair of twins. The room didn't actually grow darker, nor did the fire die, but to Pat and Jo a sudden chill descended and cast a gloom over them. The room no longer seemed home-like and cheerful. From the table the mummy grinned at them, and usurped the place of importance, the rule over everything. They tried to look away from it, but they could not.

"I wish somebody would come," said Pat.

"So do I," said Jo.

As if in answer to their wish, Yamoto reappeared bringing with him Miss Gruber. That woman hurried in, wiping her hands nervously upon her apron.

"I was busy. I didn't hear you come in," she said apologetically as she hurried to them. Her voice was tragic, almost tearful. The twins looked at her in amazement. But as they saw her sorrowful face, they realized that this expression must be her normal one, this voice her everyday voice, so deeply were the lines of grief imprinted in Miss Gruber's face. It was indeed so. Although life had not dealt harshly with Emma Gruber, she was a woman of tragedy. Each little sorrow was magnified until it reached the proportions of a major catastrophe. The burning of a roast in the oven meant to her the ill-will of a fate that was always against her. Not only was she imposed upon by fate, however, but by everybody about her. And now these twins had to come, for what other reason than to impose upon Miss Gruber? Therefore she regarded them tragically, as one would an unkind fate.

"Mr. Duer isn't here. Why he should run off at a time like this, I don't know. I suppose Yamoto's told you, though," she rasped as she bustled about the twins. "You'd better come with me to your room. It isn't going to do you any good standing here." She turned peevishly to Yamoto. "Take their bags into the bedroom. Don't just stand there, grinning like that! Oh, heavens, I wish Mr. Duer was here. Things would be different."

Grumbling and complaining, she led the way to their room, which was just off the living room. "The fire's been lit, and it's plenty warm. There's a feather bed so you won't be cold at night, although goodness knows it's cold here nights." She bustled about smoothing out wrinkles in the bed-cover that had twisted itself just to make life more difficult for her, and demean her housekeeping in the eyes of these two troublesome girls. That they would be troublesome she already knew.

"I'm sure everything will be all right," said Pat. She wanted this woman with the sad face to get out and leave them alone for a moment.

"Well, I certainly hope that everything will be all right." Miss Gruber looked as though she did not believe that it would, even that she hoped it wouldn't. If everything went right, it would almost prove that fate wasn't against her, and she was certain that it was. "And I certainly hope that you young ladies will have a good time here. Although I don't approve of gallivanting around the countryside for young girls. They're much better off at home. But I suppose everybody to his taste. You can wash up before dinner. There's hot water in that jug. Dinner's ready right away. I don't wonder it's all spoiled by now. Probably burned, or frozen cold as a stone. That's the way it is when you don't know when to expect people." She turned to go, to the relief of the two weary girls. But with her hand on the knob of the door she turned impressively and faced them.

Then she spoke in a tone of authority. "Of course, you'll remember that Mr. Duer left you in my charge. 'Miss Gruber,' he said to me, 'you're to see that my wards are well taken care of, and that nothing happens to them.' That's just what he said to me, and I hope that you'll remember that while you're here. 'And there are two things they aren't to do,' he says then.

'There are two things that they aren't to do. Under any circumstances,' he says." Miss Gruber paused to let the effect of this sink in.

Jo felt called upon to say something. "I'm sure," she said, stiffly, "that we shouldn't wish to disobey Mr. Duer's orders. What are these things that we're not to do?"

Miss Gruber looked at them dolorously, but ominously. "You're not," she said slowly, "you're not to go into Mr. Duer's study. That's one thing. And you're not to go into the woods alone. You're always to have somebody with you. Yamoto, I suppose. Although what good he is, I don't know. I never trust a heathen. If they worship idols, they'll do anything. And another thing, even though he is your guardian, I want to tell you right now that I don't put much store in your Mr. Duer and his heathen idols. This place is full of them. They don't do no good in a Christian house. But I mustn't go on like this. You two just do what I say, and you'll have a good time. I hope you do." With this final prophecy, the dismal oracle left the room.

"Well," said Jo, looking after her. "I think that we've got into an awfully queer place. If this is our guardian's household, no wonder he's odd." She turned to Pat. "Well, dear twin, don't you think that we're going to have a good time?" She expected Pat to say no, but a strange gleam came into Pat's eyes instead.

"Do you know, darling," she answered strangely, "I

think that we are. There's something awfully funny about things here. And we're going to have to get to the bottom of them. That's what's going to be fun."

"Detectiving? Not for me," said Jo. "Besides, there's nothing so strange, come to think of it, that Welton Duer has these people working for him. Of course Yamoto grins and Miss Gruber frowns, but then, you probably can't be fussy about servants in this deserted place. Poor old bachelor Welty most likely had to take what he could get up here. That accounts for Miss Gruber. And Yamoto he must have picked up on one of his expeditions. Most likely dug him up."

Pat shuddered. They were dressing for dinner, getting out of their bedraggled traveling clothes and into some soft brown fuzzy woolen dresses that they pulled out of their bags. "Don't say things like that," said Pat in a muffled voice, struggling into her dress. "Jo, no matter what you say," her dress was now completely on, and this fact made her next speech more impressive, "there's something strange around here, and I mean to find out what it is. Why aren't we supposed to go into that study? What's in there that we can't see? Jo, I mean to find out."

Jo did not fully follow the active leaps of her sister's imagination. Although she possessed normal curiosity, right now she was very hungry; therefore she was pleased when Yamoto tapped on the door and called, "Dinner!"

CHAPTER 3

The Mystery Thickens

THEY ate their dinner on a table set for two in front of the fireplace. The food was neither burned nor cold as stone. In fact, it was very good. Even Pat, forgetting her mysteries for a while, ate enormously. They didn't talk much, first because they couldn't take the time from their food (they hadn't eaten since lunch) and then because Yamoto hovered about them like a disconcerting shadow, serving their dinner. It struck them as a little odd to have an oriental servant helping them to a purely American dinner of pot roast and carrots. But serve them he did, and diligently, smiling that weird grin of his that they could not make out.

Presently, when their forks began to go with less regularity to their mouths, and they were comfortably fed, Pat looked up at Yamoto. He was pouring water into Jo's glass at the moment that Pat asked "Yamoto, what sort of man is Mr. Duer?"

Yamoto was caught off guard. His hand jerked, and

water splashed over the edge of the glass and onto the tablecloth. He recovered himself immediately, and began to mop up water with a napkin. "Excuse plees," he apologized to Jo. Jo was cheerful about it.

"That's all right," she said. "But what about Mr. Duer?"

Yamoto didn't look at them. "He nice man," he said hurriedly.

"What does he look like?" persisted Pat.

"Has he a long white beard?" This from Jo.

Yamoto turned from one to the other, grinning again. He looked relieved. "Yes, long white beard," he said. "Long, white beard."

"Is he old?" said Pat. "You know, Yamoto, an old man?"

"Yes," said Yamoto, eager to please. "Old man."

Pat went on. "He walks with a slight limp, doesn't he?"

"Yes, yes, Mr. Duer walk like this." Yamoto simulated the gait of an old man walking bent over and limping. He had quite a pretty dramatic talent. Pat watched him carefully. Jo was openly amused.

Then Pat said, "Yamoto, which room is Mr. Duer's study?"

Yamoto straightened up suddenly. "Why you want to know?" he asked. "Mr. Dluer say you shall not go there."

"Why?" asked Pat in turn.

Yamoto shrugged his shoulders. "Room over there." He pointed to a door on the same side of the room as that of the twins. "Next your room. But you no go there, huh?"

"Did Mr. Duer say that yesterday, before he took the train?"

"Yes," said Yamoto. "Before he leave he say we should tell you that."

Pat seemed satisfied. She looked very mysteriously at Jo while Yamoto was clearing the table and stirring the fire. She gave the "lot-to-tell-you-later" signal often. So often, that Jo was just as anxious as she that Yamoto leave the room. He finally did, and the relief seemed to extend to him, too. He carefully avoided any further questioning by appearing very busy, and left as soon as the fire showed signs of renewed life.

Pat watched him disappear from the room and turned to Jo.

"Well?" asked Jo. "For goodness sakes, don't act so mysterious. Tell me all."

"I will," said Pat, darkly. "Jo, there's been something dreadful going on here."

Jo was really impressed. "What do you mean?" she stammered.

"I mean this. Welton Duer did not leave this place yesterday. There was no train out of here. I thought of that as soon as Yamoto told us that he had gone. Don't you remember the schedule at the station?"

"There may have been a special train," said Jo.

"It would have been on the schedule. And the station-master would have certainly told us that our guardian had left the day before, wouldn't he?" went on Pat with invincible logic. Her face was flushed with excitement. "And furthermore, why didn't Yamoto want us to know what Mr. Duer looked like?"

"But he told us," said the practical Jo.

Pat withered her with a glance. "That's not what he looks like. Yamoto just led us on. He agreed with everything we said, so that he wouldn't have to describe him. Welton Duer doesn't limp."

"But how do you know? Is that one of the things that one just knows?" asked Jo. She did not want to be frightened by Pat's story, but the earnestness of her sister, the fire flickering on the weird animals and masks in the room, made her believe, in spite of herself, that there was something sinister in the air.

"How do I know?" answered Pat. "See for yourself, Jo. Why should a lame man, or an old man want skis? Why are those skis crossed on the wall over there?"

Jo had noticed the skis, but attached no significance to them. "Maybe they're just decorations." She was trying by logic to dispel the feeling that was gripping her. "People always have crossed skis for decorations in country houses and lodges."

"Those skis aren't for decoration," said Pat firmly.

"They've been used—often." She led her sister up to them, and together they examined the skis, which were worn smooth by use, their thongs supple and certainly not new. "You see?" said Pat triumphantly. Jo saw. There was one place in which a fastening had been almost torn through, and the tear was fresh.

"Do you suppose—Yamoto uses them?" As soon as she said this, Jo realized how funny her question was. Of course he didn't. There was only one answer left. Welton Duer was not lame and old. He must be quite spry and young—well, youngish, anyway.

"And the study," said Pat. "Why shouldn't we go in there? Isn't there something funny about that?" She clutched Jo's arm. "Jo," she whispered hoarsely, "there's something in that study that we aren't supposed to see. And I think I know what it is. Jo, can't you put all these things together? Don't you see what's happened? The train—the skis—the library? Don't you see?"

Jo didn't. Her brain, not fired with her sister's imagination, did not connect the chain of strange events. She looked to her sister, wide-eyed, for explanation. The fire was dying. She wanted to poke it up, but something kept her glued to her seat on the couch, facing Pat.

And Pat explained. "Don't you see?" she whispered. "How do you explain the nervousness of Mrs. Gruber and of Yamoto. Why did his hand shake when I asked him how our guardian looked?" Pat waited for no answer, but went on excitedly. "This is why. Something has happened to Welton Duer. They've done something to him. They've done away with him." With this awful pronouncement Pat sat back and waited for its effect on her sister.

The effect was all that could be hoped for. Jo's eyes widened still further, her mouth dropped open, the muscles of her face stiffened. "They've done—what?"

"They've done away with Welton Duer—murdered him."

"Oh, no," said Jo. "Oh, no. Why, why should they? Pat, you're imagining things." But her frightened glance furtively swept the room. The mummy's head was grinning at her. He had turned around to face them, she thought in horror, and the hair stood up on her head. No, somebody must have turned him around. Somebody must have. He couldn't possibly turn himself. He couldn't.

Pat was stirring the fire. She heaved another log into the fireplace, and manipulated it with the poker and tongs until it began to catch. Pat had lived through situations like this many, many times, so that naturally, this one did not floor her as it did Jo. Pat could stir the fire. When the log had begun to burn, she sat down next to her terrified twin. There was a smudge of soot across her nose. "I've figured it out," she said. "I've been thinking it all out carefully. They did it on account of us. It's all connected up with us."

"With us? How?" Jo managed to say. They were both taking for granted now the fact that Welton Duer had been done to death. They were ferreting out motives, now.

"They want our money. They're all in the scheme. That Gruber woman, Yamoto, and—the stationmaster. Why do you suppose he was so interested in us today? Oh, they all know about it. They're all one gang. I don't think that our guardian invited us up here at all. They invited us."

"But why?" Jo was being particularly dense, thought Pat. Couldn't she tell?

"For our money, of course. They want to get hold of our money."

For just a moment, Jo doubted. She didn't see how the murder of Welton Duer was necessary for that. In fact, she had the feeling momentarily that there wasn't a great amount of money to be got hold of. The twins had never concerned themselves with financial details. They had received a regular allowance, which increased automatically as they grew older, and had somewhere got the idea that on their eighteenth birthday, their money would be turned over to them to handle as they pleased. Outside of this, the question of money did not worry them.

So Jo asked, rather vaguely. "How are they going to do that?"

Pat waved details aside with a grand sweep of her hand. "They've worked it out. Those people always do. There's probably a will, or something. Some sort of paper, anyway." Pat got up and stood with her back to the fire, which was now blazing briskly. She planted her feet wide apart and crossed her arms on her chest, looking, she thought, masculine and authoritative. Jo recognized her as the master of the situation. She did not realize that the real master of the situation was her own fatigue. So tired and worn-out she was by the day's events, that her weary brain was willing to fasten itself to any idea, and cling.

She said weakly, "Pat, what are we going to do?"

Pat pointed impressively to the study door. "First, we're going in there."

Jo's eyes followed the pointing finger. "In there? But—"

"But no 'buts'," said Pat with finality. "We're going to search the study for—"

"For what?"

"For the corpse—or—well, for the remains. Or for some clues."

"I can't go in there," said Jo. She felt that she really couldn't. She didn't feel equal to a corpse. "Let's go tomorrow morning. Let's do that, Pat."

"Don't be cowardly, Jo. Tomorrow may be too late."
Pat added this last darkly. "Come on."

She started for the study. Jo got up stiffly and followed. She wasn't going to let Pat go in there alone.
"The door's probably locked," said Jo.

Pat stopped short. Then she said, "We'll try the key
from our door." Quietly she slipped over to their bedroom and took the key from the door. "It might work,"
she whispered. Like two housebreakers, they tiptoed to
the study, Pat a little in advance, Jo a shaky but faithful
shadow. But they never tried that key. Just as they were
about to insert it in the lock, there was a slight noise behind them. They whirled around. Yamoto, grinning his
broadest, was standing behind them. He either did not
see, or pretended not to notice, what they had been
doing.

" 'Scuse, Mliss," he said politely, and walked past
them, took a key from the bunch he held in his hand,
inserted it in the lock, opened the door, and walked in,
closing it carefully behind him. There were some muffled sounds from inside, then the door opened again, and
Yamoto came out. In his arms were a bundle of clothes.

Pat blocked his way, apparently by accident. "What
have you there, Yamoto?" she asked.

"Clothes," said Yamoto. "For washee," he added.
"Mlister Dluer say I should make clothes clean." He
sidestepped Pat, and walked quickly and noiselessly out
of the room.

Pat grabbed Jo's arm. "There go some clues," she said. "He's destroying evidence."

Jo was leaning now against the door, her hand resting on the knob, the picture of utter dejection. Suddenly her expression changed to one of amazement. She looked down at her hand, and then up at Pat.

"Pat," she said, "the knob is moving. Yamoto forgot to lock the door when he went out. Look." She pushed on the door. It opened. But Jo pulled it shut immediately.

Pat was elated. "There's nobody coming," she whispered. "We can slip in now."

Jo took her hand off the knob and let Pat open the door. A wave of cold air hit them. There was no fire in there, and it had the dank atmosphere of a closed room. "Shut the door," whispered Pat, "and I'll turn on the light."

Jo, shivering, closed the door behind her. After a short interval that seemed very long to Jo, Pat found the light and turned it on. She was glad that there was electricity, anyway. They looked around the room. It was in disorder, but it seemed a disorder of long standing. There were books everywhere, in the bookshelves that lined the walls, on the desk, on the chairs, on the floor. And scattered about with the books were papers, pages of typewritten manuscript, scraps of paper that evidently contained notes, and old newspapers.

"Where shall we start?" asked Pat helplessly. Here

was a wealth of clues, if she could get to them, but she was willing to give up her leadership at this point. Just then her eyes rested on a curiously carved chest that stood over by the far window. It looked more mysterious than anything else in the room. "Look, Jo," she said. "That chest. Let's open it."

They went over to it. But it was fastened securely. "Maybe we can force it," grunted the girl. She was trying with all her strength to pull up the lid. Jo dropped on her knees beside her.

"We shouldn't be doing this," she whispered.

"We must," breathed Pat, and pushed again. So intent were they upon their work that they did not hear the door open. There was a scream. Together they turned, bumping heads in their haste.

Mrs. Gruber stood in the doorway. She was wringing her hands, and staring at them with tragic, horrified eyes. "You mustn't touch them bones!" she wailed. "You mustn't touch Mr. Duer's bones!"

"Bones!" gasped Pat.

"Bones!" gasped Jo.

Mrs. Gruber clapped her hands over her mouth.

Then Mrs. Gruber found tongue. "I'm surprised at you, great big girls like you, not knowing how to behave. Mr. Duer's going to be mad, I tell you. And I'll tell him, too. Imagine! You weren't to come in here at all. Sneaking around as soon as my back is turned! I never. You two just march right out of here. It's time you went to bed, anyway. I've fixed your bed for you."

Automatically the twins got up and marched. They felt dazed. Bones! But there was nothing to do but leave. They went into their room with Mrs. Gruber's voice ringing in their ears.

"That I should have to put up with this. It's a judgment upon me, that's what it is. I never should have consented to be a party to such goings on. Well, next time I'll know." Her voice trailed away.

The twins faced each other. Pat's eyes were feverishly bright. "What did I tell you? Bones in that chest! Jo, we've got to solve this mystery, and solve it fast. Everything's at stake! Mrs. Gruber's conscience hurts her already. That's why she's so fussy and nervous all the time. Listen, I've got a plan, Jo darling. We'll go to bed now, and pretend to sleep. Then when everything's quiet, we'll go into the study and force that chest. We'll get something heavy to pry it up with."

"All right," said Jo and yawned.

Pat yawned, too. Mystery or no mystery, they had had a hard day. They undressed quickly and got into bed. The bed was warm and soft. At first they talked to each other to keep awake, but their voices trailed off into silence. Treacherously their eyes closed. They jerked them open again. But there was that time when those eyes refused to open once more, and almost simultaneously, the twins fell asleep. Pat stirred uneasily. Was someone in the next room? Was there really the sound of some heavy pieces of furniture being moved around? Her consciousness would not respond. Sleep conquered, and Pat did not know whether she was dreaming or not.

It must have been very early when she woke up and looked out of the window. There was just enough light to see the forms of the trees black against the snow. Then something strange appeared. A human figure, she was sure of that. But what was that behind it? As she stared, the picture resolved itself. Yamoto, dressed in his long black coat, wearing his inevitable stiff derby, was walking towards the woods, and behind him, dragged along by a rope held in one yellow-gloved hand, was a sled, and on the sled was the chest. So she hadn't been dreaming! They were taking the evidence away. They had moved the chest out of the study and were taking it to the woods to hide. No wonder the twins had been warned not to go into the woods. Well, warning or no, they would go. They'd find the chest. They'd follow the prints of Yamoto's sled in the snow. Pat was all for jumping out of bed and following him now. She pushed the covers back. It was cold in the room. She pulled the covers on again and nestled in the bed. Perhaps it would be better not to follow Yamoto right away. He'd turn around and find her. And she had better not wake Jo now. She was sleeping too soundly. The sled tracks would keep. They'd be pretty deep. Pat went back to sleep.

When she woke up again, there was a fire burning brightly in the fireplace. The room was warm, and there was the sound of voices in the next room. Nice voices. A man's and a woman's. They were talking to Yamoto.

There was a timid knock on the door, and Yamoto's voice said, "Mliss Platicia. Mliss Josephline. Lady-man to see you."

Jo was up now, too. "Who do you suppose?" said Pat.

Jo stretched and yawned. "Golly, almost ten-thirty. I had a marvelous sleep. We'd better get up and see who's here. Say," she added, as she slipped into her clothes, "weren't we silly last night? Snooping around the study! No wonder Mrs. Gruber was angry. Such nonsense!" Sleep and rest had settled Jo's fears. Daylight helped, too. She was her normal, practical self again.

But then, thought Pat, she hasn't seen what I've seen. She decided to say nothing about the sled and Yamoto. That would keep until later, and she was anxious to get into the living room and see the owners of the two civilized voices that had come out of the wilderness to call on them so early in the morning. "Ready?" she said to Jo.

"Yup," said Jo, and together they went out to greet their guests.

CHAPTER 4

The Cabin in the Woods

THE sun had quite risen when Yamoto stopped at the little hut in the woods and knocked. He knocked again, but trained servant that he was, no less politely. His courtesy was rewarded, and the door opened to him. He went in. It was cold in there. So cold that Welton Duer, after getting up to open the door went back to bed and pulled the covers back over him.

"Thank heavens you came early, Yamoto. Be a good man and make a fire. It's freezing in here. Did you bring me anything to eat?"

"Bring your bones, Mlister Dluer."

Welton Duer looked his despair. "I ask for meat, and you bring me bones. Well, stir about and make me some breakfast. Anything. Only not sardines. I had sardines last night."

Yamoto hurried around silently, but efficiently, and soon a fire was lighted in the small stone fireplace. In no time at all there was a fire in the oil stove, too, and soon after, the grateful fragrance of coffee.

"Where did you find the coffee, Yamoto? I looked all over. It's a precious time I've been having here, Yamoto, turned out of my own house. You might tell Mrs. Gruber that I miss her cooking, and that I forgive her all her weeping and wailing. By the way, Yamoto, why did you bring the bones?"

"Young ladies want to look inside last night," said Yamoto, breaking eggs into a bowl. There was butter sizzling in a frying pan.

Welton Duer snorted. "In my study already, eh? Bah! Women!" he added. "Did they want to clean it up, Yamoto? Did they throw away my papers and put away my books?" Mr. Duer was rather excited. "Keep them out, Yamoto. For heaven's sake, keep them out. It's not enough for them that they drive me out of my house, but they must go prying around in my study. Keep them out, Yamoto."

Yamoto said nothing. He watched the toast very carefully, and when it was a golden brown, buttered it thickly. Yamoto was wise. Deeds, not words, was his motto. He knew that Welton Duer could be approached in a few moments. After breakfast. So he laid the rough wooden table deftly and quickly, so that nothing had time to get cold, and summoned his lord and master. Welton Duer ate his breakfast in silence, but it was a good breakfast, and had the very effect that Yamoto intended.

He sat back and took the pipe that Yamoto had filled for him. "Grand breakfast, Yamoto," he beamed. "How you manage to get a breakfast like that out of the odds and ends around here, I don't know. I had sardines last night." He could not get over this grievance. "The key broke while I was opening the can, and I had to scoop them out in a very unpalatable mess. I ate them, though. I was hungry. How about bringing in that chest, Yamoto? I might as well get some work done while I'm exiled out here."

Yamoto went out, and Welton Duer went over to the fire to feed it some wood. He was a very tall man when he stood up, tall and slender, and had to stoop over quite far when he threw the wood on the fire. For a corpse he was very hale and hearty, and the broad shoulders told of a reserve of strength that his slender frame concealed. The fire blazed up merrily as the dry wood caught. It made his tanned skin grow ruddy, added touches of light to his brown hair, which was abundant and healthy-looking, and receded only a little on his broad forehead. He was not a young man, but still youngish, and no doubt looked younger than he really was. His beard, since he had not shaved yet that morning, was bristly, but not long, and by no means white. His eyes, however, were his best feature, grey-blue, very bright, very keen, but now and then with strange shadows that seemed to rise behind them and transform them somehow, so that they seemed puzzled and hurt. They were noticeable eyes, arresting, the eyes of a dreamer, who sometimes could go out and fulfill his dreams. The dreams, he found, were not always worth the accomplishing, and then the eyes would be puzzled and cloudy, until a new dream crowded out the memory of the old one. The new one was always much better, much more worth the danger involved. Those were Duer's eyes. The nose was not so good—not handsome, and tilted just a little at the end, which was bad for dignity. The mouth was thin and not restful, wide and well-shaped.

He stood up to his full height and stretched. Yamoto came in with the chest. "Here, put it over there next the door to the cupboard. That's it." He watched his servant's lithe movements for a little while, as he cleared the table and put water on to heat for dishes. He opened his mouth several times to speak, but closed it again, evidently thinking better of the impulse. When he did speak it was only to say, "Heat some water for shaving, too, Yamoto." And that was obviously not what he had intended to say. He was thinking of something far more important than that. Finally he said, rather surlily, "Well, what are they like, Yamoto? You needn't be quite so discreet. Say something."

Yamoto grinned. "Nlice young ladies. Velly nice." Then he added, "Velly pletty, velly young."

Duer snorted. "The worst kind. Young and pretty. I've met their kind, Yamoto. We know them, don't we?

Probably the kind that say, 'Oh, an archeologist? Mr. Duer, how exciting!' Exciting! Bah! They'd say the same thing if I told them that I was a channel swimmer, or a flagpole sitter. All they mean is 'see how interested and intelligent I look when I pretend to be interested in archaeology.' Oh, we know them, Yamoto. They're all alike."

"Think maybe these young ladies dlifferent," said Yamoto, neatly polishing a dish and not looking at Welton Duer.

"Don't let yourself be fooled, Yamoto. Some of them are slyer than others, that's all. But you, Yamoto, I'm surprised at you, a philosopher, being taken in. I'd quite counted on your good sense, Yamoto." The man looked aggrieved. If he were deserted by his staunchest ally, his cause was badly weakened. "Now look—you say that they went into my study last night and tried to pry into my fossil remains in the chest here. Didn't you tell them that they weren't to go into the study? I asked you and Mrs. Gruber to tell them that."

"Yles," admitted the man. "Mliss Gluba tell them plenty times."

"Well, they went into the study in spite of what they'd been told. What traits does that show? Curiosity, deceit, disobedience, oh, I could go on forever, Yamoto." Evidently he could not go on forever, since his adjectives gave out, and he had to stop. "It's just a catalogue of the faults of all women."

Yamoto put the dishes away in the cupboard. "Nlice young ladies," he said. "Two just the same. Look just the same. Talk just the same. Nlice." He grinned. Duer looked at him in amazement. Hadn't Yamoto heard at all what he had just said? Was all this lecture for nothing? Yamoto was deserting him. The only man in the world who knew when to talk and when to be silent was breaking his faith. Welton Duer's eyes clouded. He puffed vigorously at his pipe. Women didn't smoke pipes, anyhow.

Yamoto needed further talking to. He had never known the man to be more obtuse. He went on, almost to himself, "They'd probably say that they were interested in archaeology. And you'd believe them, Yamoto," he said darkly. "They mean that they like the jewels and other toys that are dug up. Nice things for them to play with. But just suggest to one of them that she should do some actual work—work all day in a broiling sun—get bitten by a thousand insects—do all the thousand and one detailed things that go into compiling and cataloging and summarizing results—then see how interesting archaeology would be. No, Yamoto, they're useless, women are, and pretty ones are the most useless of all."

"Allee same nlice young ladies," said Yamoto. He seemed to be a man of one idea today. He annoyed Welton Duer, who turned disgustedly, and knocked the ashes of his pipe into the fireplace. Yamoto, who had straightened up the hut by this time, got cheerfully into his overcoat and stood waiting, his hat and yellow gloves in his hand. "All right?" he asked.

"You may go," said Duer. "Everything's all right."

But Yamoto did not depart immediately. He seemed to be waiting for something. Duer sensed this and turned to him. "Well?"

Yamoto grinned. "You come home—maybee?"

Welton Duer let out a noise that was halfway between a snort and a growl. Yamoto walked to the door —quickly. There were too many small objects at hand that could be hurled, and although Mr. Duer was not ordinarily a violent man, Yamoto could tell that he had been strangely lacking in oriental tact, and that anything might happen now. After his first speechless rage, Duer said what the roar might have indicated that he was going to say. That was "no."

"Velly good." Yamoto was again suave, and Welton Duer calmed down.

"Yamoto," he said. "I'm not coming back to that house until those girls are gone, and every trace of them removed. They can do whatever they please except burn up the lodge, which they'll probably do before they leave. But they're not to go into the study. Put padlocks on the door and bar the windows, but don't let them in. That's all."

Yamoto opened the door. "I come back tonight," he said.

The archaeologist sat down on the edge of the bed. Now that the room was a little more presentable he could dress and then go out for a little exercise. It was still very early. Must be about six o'clock. He ran his hand through his hair and yawned. "Bring me something to eat. Have Mrs. Gruber fix up something good and bring it out. A man might as well have something to eat, even if he is in exile."

By this time his Japanese tact had reasserted itself, and Yamoto made no mention of the exile being entirely of his master's own making. He kept that to himself. He said only, "Bling something good," and went out.

Left alone, Duer got up, went over to the stove and dipped his finger into the water he was to use for shaving. It was still warm. Warm enough to shave with, anyway. His disposition was sweetening, as it always did when he found himself alone. He was by nature solitary, and those long stretches of time when he found himself the only white man in a wilderness of blacks who could not speak his language were not a hardship to him, but rather a blessing. He had grown up alone, an only child. He had had very few friends and all were men. It was only natural, therefore, that when he met the first girl whom he wished to have as a friend, he had placed too much confidence in her, raised her to so high a pedestal that no woman could have stood upon it without feeling slightly dizzy. The result had left Welton Duer with no faith in any woman. This was unfortunate because, taken all in all, women are not so bad. And the prejudice against the pretty ones is entirely unfounded. Patricia and Josephine Faraday could have proved this to him in no time at all if he had given them half a chance. But Welton Duer was not open to conviction.

He was rather happy though, while he shaved, and because the process did not allow for singing, he hummed. He had before him the prospect of a brisk walk through the woods, and work classifying his bones in the afternoon. In the evening Yamoto would bring him some good food. He would rest and read. What a beautiful day! Women indeed. He hummed. *La Donna e mobile. Woman is Fickle. Tum Tum Te Tum Te Tum.* Then out of the corner of his eye he thought he saw someone at the window, but when he turned to look, there was no one there. An instant later there was a terrific hammering at the door, and a rough young voice calling, "Hi, Welty, let me in!"

Half-shaved, half-lathered, Welton leaped to the door and threw it open. "Dick, my boy, come in!"

Dick Prentiss came in, trailing his snowshoes in one hand, pumping Welton Duer's hand with the other. He was beaming with pleasure, his handsome face, reddened by his early morning trek, all smiles. "So here you are, you old hermit! What's the idea of hiding on a fellow! Here I come back from college especially to beat you ski-jumping, and show off all I've learned this year, and you're nowhere to be found. I was over to the house yesterday afternoon, and your man wouldn't tell me a thing." (Duer's estimate of Yamoto rose again.) "What are you doing out here anyway?"

Duer hurriedly finished up the other half of his face. It was good to see Dick Prentiss back. Dick, for all the difference in their ages, was his pal. Together they fished, hunted and played in their beloved woods when Welton Duer was up in Michigan and Dick was home on vacation. But he was loathe to tell even Dick about his exile from home, and the reason, or rather, reasons for it. After all, he hadn't seen the boy in months and felt just a little strange. College was doing things to Dick, he decided, as he looked the boy over. He was much older than he had been last vacation; he was bigger, too, taller and broader. Why, Dick must be close to six feet now! And good-looking. They'd taken the rough edges off him. This inspection all went on very rapidly, in fact, in the space of time it took Duer to say "Oh, I thought I'd come out here to get a little work done. Nice and quiet, you know. And Mrs. Gruber objects to my bones in the house, for some reason or other."

"Your bones?" laughed Dick.

"Oh, my fossils, you young idiot. I'm doing some reconstructing, cataloguing, that sort of thing."

"Enough quiet up at that place of yours, it would

seem to me," went on Dick. "But for a quiet fellow like you, the lodge is probably bedlam, and this place is plenty noisy."

"It certainly is now," said Duer dryly. "How in the world did you happen to come out here?"

"Mother asked me to," said the boy. "She's having a crowd up over Christmas and New Year's, you know. One of those house parties that she loves so. Remember how I used to hate them? I used to sneak over and stay at your place as often as I could."

Welton Duer interrupted him. "What's this got to do with your finding this hut? How you digress, Dick."

Dick laughed. "Got anything to eat? I came out before breakfast." He found a tin of crackers and began to munch them. "Well, you see, it's this way. You probably forgot that these huts in the woods are used for stopping-off places for hikers, and for picnic spots for the summer visitors."

"I forget?" smiled the man. "I forget how the grand woods are overrun with those devastating, all-present vacationists?"

Dick took another cracker. "I knew you hadn't forgotten. I was just leading into my story."

"It's taking you a long time," said Mr. Duer.

"Oh, Welty, don't talk like a Dean. Anyway, Mother knew that some of our guests would want to hike in the woods, and she thought it would be nice if I fixed up a couple of the huts for them, stock them with food, and all that sort of thing, so that they could have something to eat when they stopped off here. Good idea, eh what? But here I find that you've usurped the best hut for yourself, and spread your bones all over the place. But thank goodness you've stocked it with food, too. I'm starved."

"So that's what brought you out before breakfast. Well. How did you leave college, Dick?"

Dick looked up quickly, and almost spluttered cracker crumbs. "Just in time," he said.

"Just in time? Come now, what have you been doing?"

Dick stood up and brushed cracker crumbs carefully onto the floor that Yamoto had just swept clean. He went over to the fire and kicked at the logs. Then he shot a quick glance at his friend, who was trying to look severe. "Now, it wasn't anything very serious," said the boy. "But you know how authorities are. They wanted to sack me, and I had to talk them out of it. It took a lot of talking, too." Dick grinned at the memory of it.

"Well, what did you do? Steal the Dean's gate and tie a cow in the chapel belfry?"

Dick snorted. "That's what they used to do in your day, Grandpa."

It was Duer's turn to snort. "I'm not so old, I can still make you take two out of three falls."

Dick measured the man with his eye. "Maybe you

could, maybe you could. We won't try now. Anyway, I didn't tie a cow in the belfry. My special crime required much more genius than that. You see," Dick sat down on a straight chair and leaned back against the wall. He enjoyed, as do all men, young and old, the relating of his misdeeds. "You see, Welty, it was this way. The night watchman out at school was giving all the fellows nervous prostration. He is just one of those meanies who likes to make trouble. He'd snoop around and if he saw any of the boys coming in late, he'd report them to the Dean. It wasn't any of his business. He was there to watch the campus. But it gave him greater joy to tell the Dean that some poor egg had stayed out after hours than to catch fifty housebreakers. Well, that kept up for a long time, and we decided that Greeny had been giving us nervous fits long enough. It was time we gave him one. Really, Welty, I don't see why we stood it that long."

"I don't see, either. Did you ever try coming in on time? That would have foiled your evil watchman. He wouldn't have had any one to report, and he'd probably have become bored and resigned in chagrin."

"I don't think we ever thought of that. You are a genius," said Dick. "Anyway, I was the first one to think up a plan. If I hadn't, somebody else would have, so I don't take any credit upon myself except for promptness."

"Don't be modest, Dick. I know that you think it was a wonderful idea."

Dick grinned. "It wasn't bad. The whole gang of us met up in Butch Martin's room and fixed it up. I put on Craley's long black coat that'd been batting around the place for a couple of years and was just a little green and moth-eaten. Then I put on some false whiskers that I'd got down in the dramatic club's property room, and some dark glasses. I think it was Butch who put the finishing touches on by blackening a couple of my teeth. But the real finishing touch, the one that almost finished me, was the hat. Remember old Pride and Joy—the green felt that I wear around here? Well, I put on old Pride and Joy and pulled it down over my eyes, and let me tell you, I was enough to make the stoutest heart quake.

"Well, I sneaked down the back stairs of the dorm after it got dark, and over behind the chapel, where it's pretty much deserted. In a little while, there comes Greeny, marching along, swinging his club, at peace with the world, and dreaming about nice boys he could report for being late. Well, just as he came opposite me, I shuffled out of the shadows, muttering and mumbling to myself. I remember that what I was mumbling was 'So, Greeny, you will doublecross my pals, will you? Well, Greeny, you're good and scared now, aren't you?' But of course, Greeny couldn't hear what I was saying. And was he scared? Even in that light I could see him turn pale. I didn't stop, though. Went right on, muttering and mumbling. When I got out of sight, I tucked up my coat and ran. That was enough for that night. I was just giving him a taste of what was coming.

"The next night I went out to the same place. Jumped out at him from behind the chapel. Well, maybe Greeny thought he'd been dreaming the night before, but this was real. He dropped his club and stood gawping at me. When I'd got a little past him, I turned and stared at him, and shook my fist. Greeny ran. I never thought Greeny could run that fast. Well, after he was out of sight, I picked up a stone and smashed a window in the Chemistry Building."

"You what?" Duer, who had been lighting his pipe, stopped with the match halfway to the pipe.

"That was my trademark. I wanted everybody to know that I'd been around. They knew it next morning. They asked Greeny about the broken window, but he said he hadn't seen anything, or heard anything. The next night there was another window broken. Still Greeny wouldn't admit that he'd run away. He began to get the jitters. He didn't go near the chapel, but I changed my hiding places, too. Jumped out at him from all sort of places. There was one good result. Greeny was so worried that he forgot to report any of the boys coming in after hours. We felt pretty cocky over our plan. Greeny was getting into hot water over the broken

windows, and the boys could come in any time they
wanted to.

"I guess we got too cocky. Anyway, after about a
week of this, I was standing in an angle of the Gym-
nasium Building, when I heard Greeny coming along.
I shuffled out, and imagine my surprise! Greeny had
brought reserves with him! Bundy the constable was
there stamping along beside him, and if you knew
Bundy, you'd know right now that the game was up.
Bundy's six feet three, and broad, and he's been chasing
college boys for years. I looked at Bundy, and Bundy
looked at me, and he knew right away that I wasn't a
ghost, or a crazy man, and I knew that I'd better run.
So I ran, with Bundy after me, and Greeny after
Bundy. Lucky for me, Bundy's not as young as he once
was, and not such a good runner any more. I hopped a
fence, and lost them. But I lost something else, too.
My hat. Old Pride and Joy sailed off and let itself be
picked up by Bundy and Greeny. After all I'd done for
that hat! We'd been pals for years and years. Well,
my initials were on the headband, and there was only
one 'D. P.' in the school, and that was me. I told the
Dean I'd pay for the windows—I'd intended to do that
all along. In fact, all the fellows chipped in and paid
for them. But the Dean felt that I ought to wear more
sackcloth and ashes than that. The old Christmas spirit
prevailed though, and I talked him into letting me
have another chance. He told me to spend my vacation

thinking over my crimes, and repenting. So that's my vile past, Welty. Do you think that you can accept me anyway?"

Duer looked speculative. "Perhaps. But I think that we'd better spend your vacation working off some of your excess energy, so that you don't go back to annoying the faculty and night watchmen. How about some good hikes, and a little skiing, or a little fishing, through the ice? Does that sound good?"

Dick was all enthusiasm. "Good? It sounds great! I've been waiting a long time for this. I never realize how much I miss you and the fun we have here until I get back and find it all waiting for me." Then his voice changed. His face fell. "But mother will be wanting me to entertain her guests. It's precious little time we'll have together." Then he brightened again. Dick could not be unhappy for more than five minutes at a time. "I'll manage to sneak out, though. You just see. I'll run over to the lodge and rout you out bright and early."

It was Duer's turn to look deflated. "Oh, you mustn't do that," he said quickly. "You must come out here for me."

Dick stared at him. "You don't mean that you're actually living out here all the time? You don't even sleep at home? What's the idea of that?"

"I like it," answered the other, remembering all the while that he did not.

"You do not," Dick told him. "Now, listen, Welty, what's your dark secret? Are you withholding things from Dickie? Out with it, what are you doing out here?"

Welton Duer puffed deliberately on his pipe before he answered. Then he said, "I've been put out of my house. Exiled."

"Put out? By whom? Yamoto or Mrs. Gruber?"

"Neither. By two women. Two young women."

"Good heavens! How did they get there?"

"I invited them."

Dickie couldn't make it out. "If you invited them, you wanted them. And if you wanted them, how did they put you out of your own house?"

Duer waved his pipe about in explanation. "It's this way, Dickie. I wanted them and then after I invited them, I didn't want them. Oh, hang it all, I may as well tell you the whole story. You've heard me mention my two wards, the Faraday girls. A few weeks ago I was sending them their regular allowance and thinking about them. My conscience began to hurt me. I felt that I hadn't been doing enough for them. Just taking care of them financially wasn't all they needed. But you know how busy I've been—and my expeditions and all—and you know how I feel in general about women."

Dickie nodded emphatically. How his friend felt about women in general amused him.

"Well, the upshot of weeks of thinking was the plan to invite them here for their Christmas vacation, and be a friend to them, and all that sort of thing. I regretted the invitation as soon as it was sent off, and hoped they couldn't make it, but they could. And Dickie, as soon as I found out that they were definitely coming, I got cold feet. I knew that I wasn't equal to facing two women at once. Of course, they're young, but they're women. So I moved out here, bag and baggage. That's the story."

"Well, of all the—" began Dickie, and then stopped short. "Do they know you're out here?"

"No!" thundered Duer, turning savagely to the boy. "And they're not to know, either, do you hear, Dickie?"

"All right, all right. Say, how old are they, Welty?"

"Sixteen. Nearly seventeen, I guess. Twins."

"Pretty?"

"How do I know? Yamoto's smitten. I don't know Yamoto's taste in such matters."

Dick was pleased. He took a few dance steps around the room. "They're sent from heaven, Welty! They're going to be the making of my vacation! Mother can have her old guests. I'm going to tell her about the twins, and have her invite them to our Christmas Eve party! Oh sing, ye sinners." He stopped whirling. "You've got to come, too. This is ridiculous, Welty, hiding yourself out here. Why, you'll perish!"

Welton Duer said no. He wouldn't come back now.

He couldn't. He didn't want to. And many things like that.

"You're a coward," said Dick cruelly.

The man acknowledged that. "Maybe I am, Dick. Maybe I'm hiding my fear behind a mask of contempt. I say that I don't like women when I'm really afraid of them. But that doesn't make the circumstances any different. I can't go to the lodge, and it doesn't make any difference if it's because I'm afraid, or because I hate women. So that's that, Dick. You run along. Get your mother to invite the girls to your party. I don't doubt that they'll like the idea."

"I like it myself," admitted Dick.

"And I can spend Christmas Eve in my own home. If you get my wards out early enough, I can go back to the lodge and spend a quiet evening alone. And now you'd better run along and get your breakfast. I'm going out for a bit of a hike."

Dick picked up his belongings from various parts of the room. He looked in the cracker box for the last cracker, but it was gone. "I'll dash home and see Mother," he said. "Mother's driving into town to get some supplies for the party. I'm going to chop down the tree. I've got it picked out already. A little beauty. On the way to town we'll stop off and get our guests invited. I know mother'll be pleased." Dick was going on at a great rate, as he struggled with the zipper on his jacket.

"How do you know that you'll like these young women?"

Dick laughed. "All young women are nice, if you'd only let yourself see them in an unprejudiced light, you old fogy. Anyway, I trust Yamoto's judgment." Dick was ready to leave. "I wish you were coming, too. You'd have a good time at the party. It would get you out of your rut."

Welton Duer snorted. "Get out of here, you young whippersnapper. I'm in no rut. And if I am in one," he went on inconsistently, "I like it. It's a very comfortable, pleasant, and solitary rut, and I don't want to be jogged out of it. Now run along. I think that college has made you very impudent."

Dick tried to look penitent. "Sorry," he said. "Didn't know you were so fond of that old rut. I'll not try to budge you again. I promise."

Duer laughed. "I'm getting old. That's what's the matter with me. Just leave me to my bones and my pipe, my boy. They'll do."

"And your slippers and cane and spectacles. You are old, my man." Dick was putting on his snowshoes outside the door, and letting in quantities of cold air.

"Get out and shut the door," shouted Duer. "I'm not so old as you think!"

Dick laughed then, waved his hand in an exaggerated farewell, and slammed the door—just in time. Duer watched him swinging off through the woods and bit on his pipe. Then he went back to the fire, kicked it up from glowing brightness to leaping little flames, and stared at it for a long time. Being of a volatile nature, however, he soon lost his air of thoughtfulness, and began to hum a little. He went over to a table in the corner and looked at some pages of manuscript, sat down on the edge of the table to study them better, his brow knit over a problem. He forgot Pat and Jo, Dick, Yamoto, all of them. In fact it was hours later before he came to, in a welter of papers, and realized that the fire was out, and that he had intended to take a hike through the woods. He yawned and stretched. "Well," he said, "so I am in a rut. Dickie was right. But it is a pleasant one." He began to thrash around, looking for his flannel shirt—his sweater. How he missed Yamoto at a moment like this. Then he found them. Bless Yamoto. He'd brought him out his warmest sweater. Welton Duer was rather happy as he went out into the biting cold air. It had been snowing. He hadn't noticed that. Yamoto's and Dick's tracks were entirely covered. He swung off into the woods, with quite a young— well, youngish, stride.

CHAPTER 5

Pat Takes the Trail

DICK PRENTISS always accomplished what he set out to do. It didn't take him long to persuade his mother that Welton's wards would be a valuable addition to their house party, and by ten-thirty she was sitting in the living room of the lodge, watching her favorite and only son stretching his legs in front of the fireplace, and waiting for Pat and Jo Faraday to come out to receive them. When Pat and Jo came out, Dick felt that all was well, and silent congratulated Yamoto on his good taste. He also commented to himself on Welton Duer's idiocy. And when the two came toward them, and smiled, bewitchingly, he knew that he must show his friend the error of his ways and bring him home. If there were any women who could show Welty that women were charming, they were these two, he thought. He sensed immediately that here were two natural good sports who would be indeed the making of his Christmas vacation.

Mrs. Prentiss introduced herself and her son. Pat and Jo brightened. What fun finding these jolly-looking people way up here in the woods. They decided, along with Dick, that their Christmas vacation was going to be rather fun—and only Pat added the reservation—when the mystery was cleared up. She had dedicated herself to the solving of the disappearance of Welton Duer, and to the purpose of finding him— or his remains. So to her, the coming of the Prentisses meant not only added pleasure but just two more people to furnish clues in her search.

Mrs. Gruber was setting the table for breakfast, slamming plates down very emphatically in protest of the twins' late rising, and the Prentiss' early calling. But Jo was entirely oblivious of any unusual ill-will on the housekeeper's part. Almost that soon had she accustomed herself to the dour nature of Mrs. Gruber. She turned to her.

"Will you set two more places, please, Mrs. Gruber?" And then to the Prentiss', "You'll stay to breakfast, won't you?"

"Sure" said Dick, who had had only two breakfasts that morning.

"Just coffee," smiled Mrs. Prentiss. She too, felt that she was going to like these two fresh young wards of Mr. Duer, and Mrs. Prentiss' standards were more exacting, and made after more mature deliberation than her son's.

The four were soon talking like old friends over the coffee cups. The twins accepted—with pleasure—the invitation to the Christmas Eve party.

"Of course," said Mrs. Prentiss, "you'll stay for the night. Half the fun of the party will be on Christmas morning when we open our gifts. We all exchange gifts—that is, little amusing things that we think are especially appropriate. We'll have to see that Santa gets your names, my dears." Mrs. Prentiss smiled.

After all the arrangements had been made, Yamoto, who had served the breakfast, came in to clear the dishes. Mrs. Prentiss turned to him. "Yamoto," she said, "it's too bad that Mr. Duer isn't here. I was going to ask him if I could borrow you and Mrs. Gruber to help out. There seems to be nobody in the village who can come. Now, do you think that it would be all right for you to come anyway?"

Yamoto considered this carefully. "I think maybe all light," he said. "I tell Gluba. She come, too."

"I don't like to act in so high-handed a manner," said Mrs. Prentiss. "I'd certainly have come over while Mr. Duer was here. But I had no idea that he'd be going away. He goes away so seldom—that is, except when he's on an expedition."

Pat looked up, all ears. "Doesn't he go away very often?"

"Why, no, he's quite fond of this home of his. Mr. Duer likes his comfort, doesn't he, Yamoto?"

Yamoto grinned, and Dick positively laughed out loud. His mother turned to him. "Why, he does, Dick. What's so strange about that?"

"I just thought of something funny," said Dick.

They all let that suffice. Except Pat. She went on with her questioning. She addressed Dick, who had managed to become sober again. "You've told us that you and Mr. Duer are great friends. Did you see him since you came home on your vacation?"

Dick blushed. "Well, you see," he began; then remembering his duty to his pal, he said bluntly, "why, no, of course not. I got home yesterday, and Yamoto told me that he'd gone. I was pretty hipped about it. I'd planned on having some pretty good times with Welty this vacation." Dick had been caught off his guard by the question, but now that he had recovered himself, it was smooth sailing. He smiled pleasantly, "But I think that old Welty's left some good substitutes for himself. I think that I'm going to have a pretty good time after all."

Dick meant this to be a gallant compliment. Jo took it as such and smiled her appreciation, but Pat, who had been watching him very carefully, saw that momentary confusion, attached great significance to that blush. Dick Prentiss, too?

"I think it's funny, too," said Pat. "Mr. Duer's going away, that is." Out of the corner of her eye she watched Yamoto leaving the room. Then she leaned over the table confidentially and said, "I think that something has happened to him."

Mrs. Prentiss looked puzzled. "Happened to him? Why, my dear, what could have happened to him?"

"He's been murdered. They've murdered him."

Her remarks had an electric effect. Dick choked. His mother sat up very straight and raised her eyebrows. Then she relaxed and laughed. "How funny you are. For a moment I thought you were serious. Why, what a fantastic idea. Murder is much too exciting a thing to have happened to our neighbor. He is really a very mild man, for all his adventuring. What a funny child you are."

Pat smiled slowly. Very well, it was a joke. They could all desert her, but she'd see this thing through. She'd track down the murderers if it was the last thing that she did.

"Why, nobody'd murder old Welty," said Dick. "I'm positive. You don't know how positive I am." He looked very solemnly at Pat.

Pat raised her eyebrows. "Positive?" she said. Then she added, "He was supposed to have left the day before yesterday. There wasn't a train out of here that day."

Dick didn't wink an eyelid. "That's nothing. Martin down at the station can wire ahead and have a train stop. You know, there are lots of trains that pass the Cove, even if they don't take the trouble to do any-

thing more than toot. They toot very haughtily, too.
You should hear them." Dick was off on a story of the
various moods expressed by the tooting of the trains
that passed the Cove. Pat did not listen to Dick's story,
but watched his face so intently that the boy grew more
and more embarrassed, and finally, beginning to stam-
mer and forgetting what he was going to say, he stopped
altogether.

To say that Pat was enjoying herself to the utmost
is to put it mildly. She was deeply involved in a
mystery. Her fanciful nature was having full play, and
she loved it. But to say that Dick Prentiss was enjoying
himself is to exaggerate. He was extremely uncomfortable under the stern gaze of Pat; his otherwise frank,
truthful nature rebelled at having to cover up his
friend Welty's weird behavior with a pack of lies; and
he hated it. Breakfast was over. What were they hanging around for? So Dick said, "Well, how about our
starting out, Mother? I'd better get going if I want to
get our Christmas tree cut. I've a good idea which one
I want. I've been watching it for years with this in
mind." Then Dick had a bright idea. What a lark if the
girls would go with him. If he couldn't have Welty
with him, he'd take the wards. Once they got out into
the air, Pat would surely lose that queer obsession
about Welty's untimely death. He almost chuckled to
himself as he thought of the grand time he'd have telling the old fellow about it. He might even, he consid-

ered for a moment, lead them to the cabin in the woods
and let them discover Welton themselves. But he put
that unworthy thought out of his head as soon as it
popped in. The least he could do was to respect his
friend's peculiarities. Duer was a good sport—there
was no man he liked better. If he did have strange
ideas about women, well, let him have them, and the
best of luck to him. Dick decided that he wouldn't
betray him—especially to Pat, who was so convinced
that he had been murdered. First he'd have to persuade
Duer that he should come back, reveal himself, and
clear up the mystery. Until he did that, it wouldn't hurt
Pat to do a little sleuthing. What fun when she found
out that Welty wasn't a corpse, but very much alive!
Dick began to feel a little better, indeed, almost happy.

"How about the two of you helping me bring in the
tree?" he asked. "It will mean a tramp in the woods for
you. I'd like to see how you like our neighborhood.
There aren't many points of interest, no cathedrals or
movie places, but I think that I can show you a few of
nature's wonders. Would you like to go?"

"Great!" said Jo. "What had we better wear?"

"Snowshoes, and—" Dick appealed to his mother.
She recognized her cue and picked it up.

"I think," she said, "that you should wear some sort
of slacks or ski pants. They're much warmer and more
useful around here."

Jo turned to Pat excitedly. "We'll wear our skiing suits," she said. "Come on, Pat. We'll change in a second."

Pat followed her without enthusiasm. It took Jo just a moment to change into her long blue trousers, tight around the ankle, and slip on the warm navy jacket, that fastened with shiny brass buttons. She rummaged about to find her red mittens, grabbed them up, and was ready to dash out again into the living room, when she discovered that Pat was not nearly ready.

"Hurry up, slowpoke," she said impatiently. "I'm dying to get out into the woods. I have been ever since I got here. Isn't Dick a swell guy, and his mother's so grand." Jo was brimming over.

Pat paused, one leg trousered, one leg bare. "Do you know," she said slowly, "I don't think that I'm going with you."

Jo protested immediately, but Pat waved her aside. "I've got a headache," she said. "I'd only spoil your fun, and not have any myself. You go on with Dick. I've got a lot of things that I can do."

"For instance?" said Jo. She was beginning to worry just a little about Pat. Never before had Pat stuck with such stubbornness to one of her fanciful ideas.

Pat waved her hand vaguely. "Oh, things. I can read, or something. I won't be bored, really. I can see the woods some other time."

Jo faced her sister squarely and laid her hands on the girl's shoulders. "Listen, darling, you're not going to do anything silly if we leave you alone?"

Pat laughed. "Trust me, Josie. I'll be a little lamb while you're gone and run up and wag my little tail in joy when you return with the tree, and I'll even baa for you."

Jo laughed, too. "I can imagine you playing lamb," she said skeptically. Then she added, "Tell me truthfully, Pat, are you serious when you say that you think that Welton Duer was murdered?"

Pat looked sober, but there were still the wrinkles of a smile about her eyes. "Maybe he hasn't been murdered," she replied, "but something has happened to him, and I'm not going to rest until I've cleared up the mystery. The murder theory was my first idea, but I'm afraid I'm alone in that. But there are too many queer things going on about here that I want to explain before I'll admit that there's nothing wrong." She gave Jo a little pat. "You go along with Dick and cut down a beautiful tree. That's a good girl."

Jo snorted. "Don't good girl me. And if I come back and find that you've been into mischief, I'll—" Jo stopped. She couldn't think of any punishment drastic enough. But her sister convinced her of her angelic behavior, and Jo left the room, reluctantly it must be admitted, since she hated to do anything without her twin.

Pat felt a little alone when she heard the three of them leave with much chatter and laughter, but her spirits soon brightened. As she had told Jo, she had things to do. The first of these things was to fly into her skiing suit. Dressed, she went out into the living room. Yamoto was sweeping. He seemed rather surprised to see her and paused with his broom midway in the air.

"You no go out?" he grinned.

"No," said Pat, thinking that the answer was really as silly as the question. Of course she had not gone out. "But I'm going," she added.

Yamoto's face clouded. "Not in the woods." He started to sweep again vigorously. "Mlissee no go in the woods, huh?"

Pat didn't answer. It seemed that Yamoto would be sweeping for a long time. She had been counting on his being in the back of the house at this time, so that she could have another try at the library. But Yamoto swept blithely on. Pat was beginning to wonder if she had really seen him going out into the woods. He seemed such a delicate person, it was hard to imagine him in any atmosphere other than a heated room. But if he had not gone into the woods with the chest, why should he be so anxious now that Pat should not go? Of course it was not a dream. She went back into her bedroom for her cap and mittens. Yamoto followed her with his eyes. The girl had said nothing, but he knew that she

was going into the woods. The oriental grinned and
shrugged his shoulders. Well, he had done his best.
If she discovered Mr. Duer in his cabin, it would not
be Yamoto's fault. And it would be Mr. Duer's good
fortune to be discovered. So Yamoto was pleased all
around, and took up his sweeping happily. He even
hummed a little tune, not, as might be supposed,
reminiscent of cherry blossoms and almonds, but the
latest radio hit.

The servant had gone into the kitchen for his dusting
cloth when Pat emerged once more from her room,
dressed for outdoors. She slipped out, closing the great
door as quietly as possible. As she stepped out on the
porch she sniffed. It was cold and crisp, but there was
a slight cloudiness that might mean snow. It was good
to be out. Pat's spirits were high, and she was ready for
big things.

First she must look into the library from outside. If
the chest was in there, she had been dreaming about the
noises, and about Yamoto's strange trip early in the
morning. If it was not there—well, she was going to
find out where it was. She circled cautiously around to
the side of the house. The window was too high to reach,
but there was an old log lying nearby. With much tug-
ging and pulling, Pat got the log up-ended, and climbed
gingerly. By holding on with her fingers to the sill of
the window, she managed to look inside. At first, because of the snow light outside, she could make out

nothing. Then slowly the interior became clear. She looked at the space where, the night before, she and Jo had knelt beside Mr. Duer's bones. The chest was not there. Pat felt a little tremor of excitement down her spine. This was unfortunate, since the tremor and excitement caused her to loosen her hold on the window sill. Her unsteady ladder slipped, and down she tumbled into the snow.

But Pat was not daunted. Up she got, brushed off the snow that covered her clothes, gingerly picked out a glob that had lodged in the back of her neck under her collar, and looked about her to see if her fall had attracted attention by its noise. Yamoto was evidently on the other side of the house, because nobody appeared to see what had happened. Mrs. Gruber, she knew, was busy in the kitchen.

Well, if the racket of the fall had not attracted the attention of the Japanese, she could go on with the next step in her plan. It was obvious now that she had not been dreaming. The chest was not in the library. She had actually seen Yamoto carry it off into the woods on his sled. Her next move was simple. She would track down the imprint of the runners in the snow, and find out what had happened to the chest. Once she found that and opened it, the mystery was solved.

Whether Pat really believed their guardian had been murdered, even she didn't know. One thing was certain. There was a mystery in the air, and she was not going to rest until she had done something about clearing the atmosphere. Pat Faraday may not have been looking for a corpse, but she was looking for something, and the search promised to be interesting. She pooh-poohed the idea that the woods were dangerous. She was going into them to carry on her search, and firmly believed that all stories of their being dangerous had been made up by Yamoto and Mrs. Gruber simply to lead her off the trail. If they told her not to go into the woods, well, naturally the woods was the obvious place to do her tracking. It all seemed so easy, it was a shame to waste time.

Cautiously the girl walked over to the place where she had seen Yamoto disappear that morning. After a little searching, and with much looking over her shoulder to see whether she was being observed, she found the tracks in the snow. Now to follow them and end all the suspense. The tracks weren't very deep, but they were easy to follow. Evidently the chest was not very heavy, or the runners would have sunk deeper into the snow. She did not notice the grinning oriental face that appeared suddenly at the window, saw her enter the woods, and as suddenly disappeared.

Pat was tense with excitement. She was going toward some mysterious something, she knew not what. And it was pleasant going there. There was little wind, and the cold was stimulating, not uncomfortable. A few flakes of snow fell. When she came to a little clear space, she ran, dodging the branches of evergreen that slapped back at her and sent a fine spray of snow into her face. Her cheeks were tingling, and her nose felt cold.

She scooped down into the snow and came up with a fistful of snow, packed it tight in her mittened hands until she had an icy snowball, and tried her luck at hitting the black trunk of a tree somewhat further on in her path. She missed it by a good distance. The next one came closer. She tried a tree further on. She hit it, and her success pleased her so that she laughed out loud. In this way, playing, laughing, running, she covered more ground than she realized. The snow came down a little faster.

If Pat had had the instincts of a woodsman, she would have turned back now. But to her, the woods were not dangerous. She was used to the small woods surrounding her boarding school, where she knew every tree, every landmark, and could have found her way about in the pitch blackness of a moonless night. Because she did not know the immensity of this tree-covered land, she blissfully followed the tracks before her, which now seemed more and more difficult to make out.

Suddenly the world turned to snow about her. Down came the snow, so thick that she could not see six feet before her. It swirled angrily about and got into her nose and eyes and mouth. Pat lowered her head to escape the storm, but the snow followed her, slipping down the back of her neck, covering her hair, plastering her suit, until she was snow from head to foot.

Pat's heart sank. She looked down frantically at the ground and discovered that the tracks before her were snow-covered. She couldn't follow the marks that Yamoto had left with his sled! There was only one thing to do, turn back and follow her own footsteps back to the lodge. Quickly she turned, and began to retrace the uneven tracks made by her own feet. For a short distance she could follow them easily, but then she came to the sickening realization that they, too, were fast being covered up.

How far she had really come into the woods Pat couldn't tell. She hadn't noticed the time, being so preoccupied with the fun that she was having, and so certain that she would be able to follow the two narrow sled marks to the place where they stopped, and the mysterious chest reposed. But in her excitement she could reason that she had not come very far, since Yamoto had gone to his destination and returned before she and Jo had awakened. She felt herself suddenly wishing that Jo were with her. Somehow she relied more than she would admit on the steadiness of her twin. It wouldn't be so frightening now if only her twin were there to help her find her way out of the storm.

At the thought of Jo, Pat took heart. If she were just careful, and made sure that she kept walking straight in the direction from which she had come, she would soon find her way back to the lodge. And stay there, too, she hissed through her clenched teeth. She buffeted forward against the wind, keeping an eye out for any landmark that she might recognize. The trees on all sides looked alike, all black-trunked, snow-laden. The air was clearing a little; the snow seemed to be falling less violently, in a steady downfall, so that she could distinguish a little better the trees' grim sameness. So intent was she on searching out landmarks, that she almost forgot the cold, but now it became so acute that she could ignore it no longer.

Her hands were cold and aching, and she felt her feet stiffening in their heavy boots. It became harder and harder for her to plow through the snow on legs that were refusing to bear her up. Almost exhausted, she breathed in short gasps, and the cold air and snow drawn down her throat and into her lungs made them sore. Only the thought that she had not gone very far, and that she would soon be home, and warm and dry, sustained her. She wished that she had listened to the warnings of Yamoto and Mrs. Gruber, and not gone into the woods. She wished that she had taken Jo into her confidence, and told her where she had planned to go. This was the first time that she had ever kept anything from her twin, the first time that she had not shared every secret with her, and she was already regretting it. But now, by the time Jo came back with Dick—well, who could know what might have happened? Pat would not let herself think of that, but tumbled on.

Her fingers ached so that she pulled off her mittens to rub hands. One of the red woolen mitts dropped in the snow. Pat almost cried aloud with annoyance, but she could not stop to pick it up. If she stopped, it would be so much harder to start again, and she felt that she could not make the effort. She left the glove, a red blob on the snow, and struggled on. It couldn't be much longer now. She'd been walking back—how long? She couldn't tell, but she knew that she must be almost out of the woods. She let her mind dwell on the warm fire, on something hot to drink. She'd soon be there. With this thought to sustain her, she forced herself on. She must be almost there now. What was that on the snow before her? She came closer to it. It was her red mitten! She had been walking all this time, and was back to the place from which she had started! She was walking in circles. Pat screamed. She wasn't conscious of the sounds that came from her throat, but she was shouting for help. She had not cried out before; she had felt that shouting would be useless, since there was no living thing to hear her cries.

Now she felt trapped. She could go no further since she would be walking in circles. How often she had read of persons lost in the woods and walking in circles, each circle smaller than the last! Why should she go on like that? Pat clung to the trunk of the nearest tree and shouted. She felt her grip relaxing. She was getting very tired. And just as she was about to close her eyes, something large loomed up before her, and she fell into a pair of masculine arms.

CHAPTER 6

An Accident

Jo was a little worried about her sister when she got
into the Prentiss car that was waiting for them outside.
But then, it was so comfortable under the woolen robe
and Dick was so lively and talkative as he pointed out
landmarks all about them, that she soon forgot her
worry, and assured herself that everything was all right,
and that Pat would do nothing foolish while they were
gone. She put all her disturbing thoughts at the back of
her head and listened to Dick Prentiss.

"See that high rock?" Dick was saying. He pointed to
a long, sloping rock, snow-covered and steep.

"Yes," said Jo, a little obviously. How could she help
but see it?

"I took my first skiing lesson there," said Dick.
"Welton Duer took me to the top and let me ski down.
It was great sport."

Why did he have to mention Welton Duer? All the
little worries came back out and paraded themselves

before Jo. She was well content that her guardian had merely gone off on an unexpected trip, but she knew too that the curious and adventurous Pat was not convinced. But she mustn't let the others know that she was worrying, so she said,

"My, that's an awfully high rock."

Dick looked a little too proud. "Pooh," he said, with a little manly puffing out of his chest, "that's nothing."

Mrs. Prentiss smiled at her son. Assuredly he was growing up. She turned to Jo and said, "It certainly is a high rock. Dick was just a little boy, too. I used to worry about him when Mr. Duer had him out in the woods teaching him how to ski and skate and goodness knows what all. But I soon grew to trust the two of them. And it really doesn't seem to have done Dick here any harm, all of the rough handling he got."

"It certainly hasn't," said Jo and then blushed at the admiring glance that Dick threw her. Jo said to herself, "Be careful, Josephine. Don't let this young man think he's too good, or he'll become unbearable. Boys must be put in their places, or they begin to brag and boast and aren't pleasant at all. And this one is really so nice to begin with that I'd hate to have him spoiled." So Jo returned the admiring look rather coldly, and settled back into her corner of the car.

But Dick, exuberant and still thanking his lucky stars that he had run into such pleasant company on his vacation, did not notice the cold look and went on talking.

"There's another story about that rock," he said. "Shall I tell the one about Old Gregg, Mother?"

Mrs. Prentiss nodded. "Of course. I've heard it before, but I think that I can stand hearing it again."

"Well," said Dick turning to Jo, "Old Gregg used to imbibe a little too much on some nights, and then he'd sort of lose his way when he left the village and set off for home. Well, one night, when he was just a leetle bit—well, let's say gay and jolly, he was going home, singing to keep himself company, when suddenly he saw a peculiar light. It seemed pretty close, and Old Gregg decided that he'd go see what that light was. Well, when he went toward it, it moved away. But Gregg didn't get discouraged. He followed after. And the faster he followed, the faster that light went into the distance. Then Gregg suddenly decided that light or no light, he was tired and couldn't follow another step. He lay down just where he was and went to sleep. When he woke up in the morning, he found that he was right on the edge of that big rock. Another step and he'd have gone over and probably broken his neck."

Jo was interested in spite of herself. "Why, what do you suppose the light was? What was he following?"

Dick looked very mysterious. "We'll never know," he said. "All we do know is that Old Gregg hasn't touched a drop since that day. He says that it was a 'hant' that was luring him over the rock, and that his good angel saved him by stopping him at the edge. We don't know any different, of course, so we'll have to believe his story. Anyway, he signed the pledge and never took another drop, at least so far as we know."

"Has anyone else ever seen the mysterious light?" asked Jo.

Dick laughed. "Say, you're not trying to work up any mysteries, are you? There probably never was a light. Gregg just had a bit of good luck that saved him from breaking his neck. Leave it to a girl to try to make a mystery out of it. Sounds just like your sister Pat making a mystery out of Welty Duer's going away——"

Jo flared up. She would defend her sister against anyone. Of course, she thought that Pat was making too much of a mystery of the whole thing, but then—who was this rude boy that he could say so?

"Pat isn't making any mystery," she blazed. "She just saw the facts of Welty Duer's going away didn't jibe. You can't blame her for talking about a thing that was perfectly obvious, can you?"

Dick was taken aback. "Why, I didn't mean——" he began.

Mrs. Prentiss tried to pour oil on troubled waters. "I'm sure Dick was just joking," she said smilingly to Jo. "He loves to joke."

But Jo was not to be appeased. She said very little the rest of the trip, sitting quietly in her corner and watch-

ing the snowy scene slip by them. Her feet were getting
a little cold even under the woolen robe, and she wondered if she would ever get used to the cold in this
isolated spot. Mrs. Prentiss and Dick seemed perfectly
comfortable.

Dick was comfortable, at least, physically. But men-
tally he was suffering. "You dang fool," he said to
himself. "Now you've gone and done it. You've hurt
this nice kid's feelings, and now she probably will be
angry with you for the rest of your vacation. Well, I
guess you're just losing your tact. You don't know how
to talk to a woman any more, Dick, old boy. Now, what
can I say to her that will make her smile again?" But
scour his brain as he would, he could not think of the
magic phrase that would make Jo smile at him as she
had. In fact, the more that he tried to think of winning
words, the fewer could he think of; his brain seemed
to freeze under the chill of Jo's icy glance.

It was Mrs. Prentiss who stepped into the breach.
She began to talk about the Christmas party that they
were to have. "I think that you'll like our friends," she
said. "There is one girl in particular I'd like you to
meet, and that is Mavis Martin. I think you'll like her,
and I'm sure that she'll like you and your sister." She
turned to her son. "Don't you think that the twins will
like Mavis?" she asked.

Dick was enthusiastic. "You bet they will," he said.

His mother was a peach for taking up the conversation and getting him out of the awkward situation he'd got himself into. "Everybody likes Mavis. She's a great sport. You should see her skate." And Dick went into a glowing description of the wonder of Mavis Martin on a pair of steel skates.

Jo felt vaguely annoyed. It wasn't the same sort of anger that she had felt when she'd defended Pat. It was a different sort of feeling entirely, very slight, but persistent.

"I'm sure I'll like Miss Martin," she said at last. "She sounds just delightful." But her heart was not in her statement. She felt that perhaps she was not going to like the girl at all. She was curious to see her, nevertheless. She wanted to see the sort of girl that Dick Prentiss could find so charming and wonderful. Not that it mattered. Dick was just a rude boy. But still—

Mrs. Prentiss was still talking. "Perhaps it's frivolous to have a costume party on Christmas Eve," she said. "But I think grownups never have such a jolly time as they do at a dress-up party. And I think that Christmas Eve should be jolly, don't you?"

"Oh, it should," agreed Jo. "But I didn't know that we were to come in costume. Pat and I didn't bring anything like that, you know."

"That's all right," said the older woman. "Just put something together and make a costume. I think that

that kind is always more successful than something elaborate. You and your sister really don't need much adornment."

Jo blushed and avoided looking at Dick. "We'll find something," she said.

They were passing a thick wood.

"Here's our stop, Mother," said Dick. "I've got a beautiful tree marked for destruction. It's going to be butchered to make us a glorious holiday. I think that it will like going out in a blaze of glory, though. Just think of what a grand night it's going to have. I'd be willing to end that gorgeously," said Dick.

"Out with you," said his mother, as they stopped the car. "You're getting positively poetic, Richard. And a philosopher, too. Now, don't get too absent-minded and not take care of Jo properly. She's a city girl, you know."

Jo laughed. "I'm hard as nails, Mrs. Prentiss," she said. "If Dick gets too absent-minded, I'll lead him back to safety."

"Shall I stop by for you on my way back?" asked the woman. She added to Jo, "You mustn't do too much, or overestimate your endurance. You may be too tired to walk all the way back. It's pretty cold up here, and you might not be accustomed to it yet."

Jo thought of Mavis Martin and her wonderful prowess in sports. Not that she wanted Dick to admire her—well, not at all. But if Mavis could be such a grand sport, why couldn't she, Jo? So she said, "Oh, I assure you, Mrs. Prentiss, I won't get cold, or tired, either. I'd really rather walk back than have you stop."

Dick was agreeable, so it was decided that the two of them should hike back, and Mrs. Prentiss drove on. Dick strapped Jo's snowshoes, while she stared straight before her like a young queen being served by a lowly page. Dick, a little amused, a little angry, thought of Gareth, in King Arthur's Court, who had been treated so disdainfully by his lady, and triumphed in the end, winning her love and admiration. Well, wait until this young lady saw him cut down the Christmas tree. She couldn't withstand that. Dick shouldered his axe, and started off into the woods, searching for dragons to kill for this haughty maid.

They said little as they strode along the snowy path. Jo had a little difficulty with her snowshoes, but she would not for the world have asked for help. So she floundered about, stumbling, getting tangled up and kicking up clumps of snow, until she got the hang of the things, and the going was better.

Not that they would have spoken much anyway. The woods were so still and quiet that it would have seemed sacrilege to break the silence with words. The snow, hanging thick on the branches of the evergreens, muffled and deadened all sounds, and the crunching of the snowshoes and the occasional scurrying of some animal through the brush was all that disturbed the calmness of that tract so seldom invaded by human beings. Jo, as she watched Dick gliding before her, could not help thinking that the two of them looked like some pioneer couple going into the forest in search of a tree for fuel. Or like something on a Christmas card. She felt almost kindly toward this great boy, but then she remembered that he had maligned her sister, and that he must be put in his place, and she did not relent.

"This way," said Dick shortly and turned off the path into a denser growth. "It's off this way. I left a trail last time I was here."

Jo could not see any trail, and Dick knew that she couldn't. He pointed out, rather condescendingly, a series of gashes on the trees that they passed. "That's called blazing a trail," he explained.

"Oh, of course," said Jo. "Were you a Boy Scout?"

"I was," said Dick. "That's why I'm so good at woodcraft."

"Well," mocked Jo, "you must be good if you say so yourself."

"Watch me," said Dick. They had reached a beautiful graceful fir tree, which was evidently the one that Dick had chosen as their Christmas tree. Jo could not help but admire the tall lovely fir. She watched Dick plant himself squarely in front of the tree, grasp the axe firmly by its handle, swing it over his head and cut cleanly and truly into the trunk. His lithe young body swung the axe in a rhythmic movement, and the blow of steel on wood resounded through the forest. Dick knew that he looked splendid, and he made the most of his prowess. Each stroke fell true, and the chips made a little heap beside the trunk of the tree.

But Jo was not to be moved. When Dick paused to rest, leaning upon the handle of his axe like Abe Lincoln the rail-splitter, he very obviously called for some remark, but Jo made none, except to call attention to the fact that she hoped that the tree would fall the right way. "I'd hate to be in the way when it fell," she said.

"If you keep out of the way you won't be hurt," said Dick rather curtly. "The tree's going to fall over this way. Just move to that bush over there and stand there."

Jo didn't like the tone of his voice. She loathed being ordered about, and especially by someone who was too young to have the authority to do so. So she said, "You make your old tree fall the other way. I'm going to stand here." And she stood there.

Dick looked at her in disgust. "Will you please move over here?" he asked calmly.

"No," said Jo.

Dick went on chopping his tree. He felt sure that when the tree was about to fall Jo would get out of the way. No girl was so stubborn that she'd let a tree fall on her, he thought, as he swung the axe with vigor. One more stroke. He stood back. "Look out!" he shouted. The tree swayed, then, with a groan and a swish, fell to the earth.

Jo jumped aside. But she was clumsy in her snow-shoes, and her jump was just a little too late. The long branches of the tree caught her as they fell and dragged her to the ground.

When Dick reached her side she was looking up at him from a frame of fir boughs. Dick's face was white as he bent over her.

"Jo, Jo, are you hurt?"

Jo tried to appear dignified, but she knew that she couldn't. Dick looked so funny, and she knew that she must, too. "No," she said, "I'm not hurt, but will you please take your old tree off me?"

Dick tugged at the tree, and Jo realized then that she was hurt a little, anyway.

"For heaven's sake, why didn't you move?" asked Dick. But his voice was not angry. He had been too scared when he saw the tree toppling over on Jo to be angry with her. What a girl! He saw that he had an unusual person to deal with. And he didn't know but what he didn't like her all the better for her courage and stubbornness. Here was a person who knew what she wanted.

Jo was very much subdued when Dick had tugged the tree off her. The fir had squelched her spirits if nothing else. Nothing else? Dick was trying to pick her up, but she would have none of it. She wanted to get up herself.

That was all right until she tried to stand on her two feet, and then her left leg almost crumpled up under her. "I've hurt my ankle," she said in a small voice.

Dick didn't say "I told you so." It took great self-restraint to keep himself from saying it, but he felt too sorry for Jo and for the humiliation that she must feel to say anything like that. And how was he going to get her home? Then he had an idea.

"Say," he said, "you've got to get some rest. You can't walk all the way back on that bad ankle. You'll ruin yourself. There's a cabin a little beyond here. It hasn't been used since summer and it'll be cold, but you can rest there anyway until we see what we can do about the ankle. How about it?"

"All right," said Jo. "I'd really like to walk home though. I hate to be a bother." She tried to walk on the bad ankle, and made a wry face.

"Here, here, don't do that. You'll make it worse. Come on, I'll carry you. It isn't far."

Jo tried to object, but Dick lifted her off her feet and carrying her as though she were no burden at all, made his way back to the path down which they had come. Then he went deeper into the woods. He noticed that the sky was looking unusually dark. A few flakes of snow fell. "We're in for it," he said to himself. "We're in for a bad one." But he said nothing to Jo, not wishing to worry her.

A sudden blast of wind whipped up the snow and

blew a swirl of it into their faces. Jo buried her face in Dick's shoulder, and said in a muffled voice, "You'd better let me down. You can never carry me through this storm."

It was storming in earnest now. Dick didn't waste energy talking to Jo. He merely lowered his head to protect it from the driving snow and plunged on. The cabin must be pretty close now.

Jo didn't ask him to let her down again. She knew that she was much better off where she was, although she could feel that she was becoming heavy in Dick's arms. He was struggling through the drifts, stopping to rest every now and then when he could go no further. What if he had got off the path and they'd missed the cabin? The thought made Dick almost sick with anxiety. It seemed that they had walked a great distance. In fact, Dick never remembered having walked quite so far in his life. He didn't want to admit to Jo that he was worn out, so he plunged on, although his arms were aching. Just as he was about to admit defeat, and was laying plans for making some shelter for themselves in the storm, the cabin loomed up before them. Dick sighed with relief. "Here we are," he panted to Jo. "I'll let you down here. Can you walk now?" They unstrapped their snowshoes.

Jo found, to her surprise, that her ankle pained hardly at all. "Why, my ankle's practically all better. Let's get inside. I'm freezing."

Dick helped her over a snowdrift and pushed open the door of the cabin. He gasped in surprise. "What's the matter?" asked Jo, behind him.

"Why, why, there's a fire inside! Somebody's living in here!" For a moment Dick had had a terrified thought that perhaps they had stumbled upon Welty Duer's cabin. But immediately he knew that this was impossible. They were miles from his cabin. This one, exactly like Duer's, was also a summer cabin, used by tourists who came to visit the resort. Nobody ever came here in winter. But evidently somebody had.

Jo looked over his shoulder as they went into the warm cabin. "Anybody here?" called Dick. There was no answer. When their eyes became accustomed to the darkness of the room, they were sure that it was deserted. They closed the door behind them and looked about curiously. The place was very untidy. Clothes were strewn about and dishes stood on the table. It was evident that someone had had breakfast here and gone right out without stopping to clean up.

"A man's been living here," said Jo, going over to the fire. She was peeling off her wet clothes, and shook them out. "I'm awfully grateful to him for leaving a fire, although I don't admire his choice of a winter home. Who lives here?"

"Nobody," said Dick. "At least, nobody's supposed to be living here. All that I can figure out is that someone from the town moved out here for a while to get in a little good hunting. Whoever got the bright idea, though, gets my vote of thanks. I couldn't have gone much further, that's certain. Gosh, look at that storm."

They looked out at the storm raging outside. It was good being inside in front of a fire, with plenty of firewood to keep it going. Dick dropped into a chair.

"I'm sorry I was such a bother. I guess that trouble with my ankle was just the fact that my snowshoe thong was twisted. I suppose Mavis Martin wouldn't have done a silly thing like that."

Jo felt unutterably silly. What a nuisance she was.

But Dick was smiling. Now, safe inside the cabin, he felt kindly toward the whole world. The fire warmed his heart as it thawed out his cold hands and feet. And what a change in this girl! He was almost glad that the tree had fallen on her. Oh, no, not glad. He mustn't admit that even to himself, but it was so much pleasanter to have her friendly and jolly again. So he said happily, "Oh, I suppose Mavis got into plenty of mischief when she was young."

"When she was young?" asked Jo in surprise. "Isn't Mavis young?"

"Oh, yes, young," said Dick smiling, "but not as young as you. I'd say that Mavis was about, well, beginning her thirties. But she's the kind that will never grow any older than twenty. You'll like her."

Jo did not know why, but she felt relieved. And with her mind at rest, she began to think of other things.

"Do you suppose there's anything to eat around here? I'm starved."

"I hope there is," said Dick, "I'm sort of hungry, too. Let's make a raid."

Their raid netted them some beans and bacon. Almost all of the dishes in the cabin were dirty, but they managed to find two tin covers that served them very well as plates. When they had finished their lunch, Jo felt that they should do something in gratitude for their food.

"I'll bring some more food out tomorrow," said Dick. "The man who has this place probably counted his provisions pretty carefully. We don't want to starve him out. He's probably been caught out in the storm, and is waiting for it to clear up a bit before he starts back."

"Well, let's clean up this place. That will be part payment for our shelter," said Jo. "Here's a bucket of water. We'll heat it and wash the dishes. How about it?"

"At your service," said Dick.

The work went quickly. They had a good time over it, Jo washing and Dick mopping them with a towel that wasn't very clean. But even after the room was looking fairly neat again and their work was finished, the storm was still raging.

"It looks as though we were in for a long stay," said Dick. "We may as well make ourselves comfortable."

He threw some wood on the fire and watched it blaze up.

They sat down cozily in front of the fire. "I wish Pat were here," said Jo. "That would make things complete. I hope she isn't worrying about me. And I hope that she isn't getting into mischief. Somehow I always worry about that girl when she isn't with me."

Dick laughed. "It seems to me that both of you are good at getting into mischief."

Jo looked a little piqued, but then she laughed. "I guess we are. But you aren't allowed to say so. That is, you may say it about me, but not about Pat. We're notoriously quick to take each other's parts against anybody. So be careful, young man."

Dick promised that he would be careful. "But really, the mystery of Welty Duer; what can she be thinking of? Both of you have read too many adventure stories."

"Maybe," said Jo quietly, "but don't you believe in these things at all? Don't you think that there are mysterious powers that we know nothing about?"

Dick scoffed. He was at the stage where science was taking the leading role in his life, and fancy was being quietly subdued. "There's always some explanation for these things," he said.

"Not always," said Jo. "Now, something happened to a friend of mine that has always made me feel that some unseen force acts in our lives. Life can be very mysterious."

"Tell me," said Dick. "It sounds like a good story."

"It is," said Jo. "We haven't anything else to do, so I'll make a short story long."

They settled down, and Jo began her story.

CHAPTER 7

Stories

"KITTY FERGUSON's the vivacious type," began Jo, staring into the crackling fire. "She's awfully pretty, and so gay and witty that everybody at school adored her. That's why we were so surprised when she came back to school one year very depressed and gloomy, not at all her happy-go-lucky self. She wouldn't talk to any of us—just stayed in her room. If anyone went in to visit her she was so morose and silent that the visitor never dared to return.

"Pat finally found out this much from her—that her baby sister, whom she had worshipped since the child was born, had died that summer. Of course, that would explain her grief, but somehow it didn't explain it entirely. There seemed some awful weight bowing her down—some weight that had to be lifted before Kitty could recover her gay personality. One night Pat and I all but forced her to come into our room for some hot chocolate. It was that night that she told us her story, the story I'm going to tell you now."

Jo turned to Dick and looked at him from under raised eyebrows. "Of course you'll scoff," she said, "and say that the whole thing was coincidence. But you've got to listen, anyway."

Dick grinned. "I've come to scoff," he said, "but I may remain to pray."

Jo leaned forward and clasped her knees in her hands. "This summer Kitty spent with her family, as usual, on their country estate. Her father's friend, Mark Hewlett, came to visit for some time with them, and since Kitty's father was working in the city during the week, it was up to Kitty to entertain him. That wasn't hard to do. Mark Hewlett had been all over the world—not on the beaten track, but to all sorts of queer places. He'd seen strange sights, and done unusual things, and he could tell about them in such an interesting way that Kitty was never tired of listening to him. Then, there were such amusing things to do on the estate that the two of them had a jolly time, even though Mr. Hewlett was twice as old as Kitty.

"One day they decided to climb Sunset Hill in order to see one of the flaming sunsets that could be seen to such good advantage from the hill, and had given it its name. It had been a hot afternoon, the climb was steep, and they were pretty tired by the time they reached the top and sank down in the long grass.

"The sunset was worth it, though, and the air grew so deliciously cool after the sun went down that they just sat on in silence while the twilight drew in around them.

"Hewlett had taken a coin out of his pocket, and was aimlessly tossing it into the air and catching it again. Suddenly he grasped it tightly in his hand and stared at it. Kitty was startled at his quick movement and turned to him questioningly.

"He smiled. 'I didn't realize that I was being so careless with my magic coin,' he said.

" 'Magic coin?' Kitty waited for him to go on. It sounded like a story.

" 'I got this in India,' he said. 'It has unusual powers. If you hold this coin in your left hand and wish, your wish will come true.

"Kitty could not control the unbelief that came into her face. She looked at the man with twinkling eyes. But there was no answering twinkle in his eyes as he stared down at the coin. A strange feeling came over the girl. Mark Hewlett took this seriously!

" 'Do you wish on it?' she asked.

" 'Only one wish to a person,' he said then, looking at her strangely. 'Once you have wished, the coin loses its power, so far as you are concerned.'

" 'Have you had that wish?'

" 'No,' said Hewlett quietly.

" 'Oh, but why? I'm sure that if it were mine. I'd

have wished long ago. How can you be sure that it really works if you haven't tried it?'

" 'I'm afraid to,' Hewlett answered.

" 'Afraid?' Kitty stared at him with questioning eyes.

" 'Yes, afraid.' The man looked at her earnestly, as though he knew that she was judging him, and finding him ridiculous. 'This little coin is a magic coin, and a bad luck coin, too. Everybody who has ever made a wish on it has wished that he hadn't. Each got his wish; it seemed the thing that he wanted most at the time; but when it had been fulfilled he regretted ever having made it; and some of the regrets were tragic.'

"Kitty held out her hand for the coin, and Mark Hewlett dropped it into her open palm. It was warm and smooth, with a little chased design around the edge. 'This doesn't look very dangerous,' she said. Then, 'do you know, Mark, I think your story is very interesting, but I don't think that I believe in the power of your little coin.'

" 'You don't? I do, Kitty.'

" 'Pooh,' said Kitty, 'you admit yourself that you've never tried it. You'll never know whether it's good or not.' Then suddenly she closed her fingers about the coin and raised her arm. 'Mark,' she cried, 'I'm going to try it for you. I'm not afraid. I'm going to make a wish!'

" 'Kitty! Don't!'

"Kitty laughed and shook her head at him. 'I won't

wish anything very important. Just a little experimental
wish that won't be disappointing if it doesn't come true,
and won't hurt anybody if it does.'

"Mark Hewlett looked aghast at her. 'Kitty, give me
that coin.'

"But Kitty, grasping the coin, backed away. 'I wish—
I wish—I wish that I had a drink of water! There, I've
done it. You can have your coin.'

"Mark Hewlett took the coin from the girl automatically. 'I wish you hadn't done that, Kitty,' he said.

"Kitty laughed. 'Nothing's happened. Your coin's an
old fraud. Where's my drink of water? I guess we'll
have to go down to the house for it.'

"They started off then down the hill. Just as they
reached the little woods that extended almost to the
top of the slope, a little boy came out from behind the
trees trudging toward them. He seemed very weary,
and the little knapsack that he had on his back seemed
almost too heavy for him.

" 'Why, it's the gardener's Jimmy,' said Kitty. 'What
can he be doing up here?'

"Jimmy, they found, had just come up for a picnic
all by himself in the woods. He was very tired. And
very thirsty. He opened his knapsack and took out a
bottle of water that his mother had packed for him.

"Kitty looked at Mark in wonder. 'Here,' she said in
a small voice, 'is my drink of water.'

"She drank the water, kissed the little boy, and then

they walked on down the hill in silence. Kitty felt just a little afraid. If one part of the story had come true, why not the second? Would she really regret her wish? She shook off her unpleasant thoughts as they approached the house. Her little sister ran out to meet them. Kitty picked her up and kissed her tenderly. She loved her sister better than anyone else in the world.

"But that was a fatal kiss. The child in a few days complained of being tired; she sickened rapidly; and finally died of smallpox. The gardener's son, Jimmy, died of the same disease just a few days before her. Kitty had transmitted the disease to her sister."

Jo paused to let Dick get the best effect of the story. Then she said, "Well, what do you think of that? Now do you believe that there are supernatural forces that we cannot see but that are all around us?"

Dick smiled. "Well, it was a good story, anyway. I think that you have a wonderful imagination."

"Why, Dick Prentiss, that's a true story. Anyway, I'd like to hear you tell one as good." Jo smiled. She was perfectly willing now to sit back and be entertained.

Dick stirred the fire a little. "Well, that's a hard one to beat. Anyway, I think that I can tell you one that will make your marrow run cold. I'd better stir up a good fire."

"Go ahead," said Jo. "After all, you're an old scoffer. Just try to scare me."

"Well," began Dick, "which is the traditional way in

which people begin to tell stories. This is true, too, and it happened to a friend of mine. He was traveling over in England, and was invited to spend the week-end with a man he'd known in college over here—an Englishman who'd come over to America to study.

"His friend belonged to an old family, and lived in his ancestral home, a large rambling gray stone manor that had a lot of ghosts walking through its drafty halls —or at least, so tradition had it. It was a rainy night when my friend got there, one of those cold, damp, penetrating nights, when it's good to be inside looking out.

"Well, he went up and rang the bell, and it was answered by an old butler, who seemed as old as the house. He told the man that his master had been called out of town, but that he would be home late that night. My friend was to make himself at home until he got back. The butler showed him to his room and told him that dinner would be served in half an hour.

"The dinner was good—the food well-cooked, and my friend was feeling pretty good. He went back to his room, determined to read until the master of the house should come back.

"He tried to read, but he couldn't. The place was so strangely quiet. The servants' quarters were far away, in another wing of the building, and he seemed to be the only living being in the huge place. Out of the silence would come queer noises. You know the sort of noises that you hear when you're alone at night in a strange place. Swishing noises and scraping noises, and noises made by the knocking of bony knuckles on the wainscoting, or something equally scary. Finally he couldn't stand it any longer. The little fire that had been burning in his room went out, and he really didn't have the courage to get up and rekindle it, so he decided that about the best thing to do would be to get into bed. He could wait for his friend in bed as well as anyplace else. It would be warmer, and, well, he hated to admit it, but it would be safer.

"He had a hard time getting to sleep, but he finally did doze off. Then suddenly he woke up. There was somebody in the room. He sat up and peered into the darkness. Yes, there was somebody sitting at the foot of his bed, a bent, bulky figure, swathed in some sort of robe. It must have been a woman, and she was sewing, with long, flowing sweeps of the arm, as though her needle had been threaded with a very long thread, and she had to draw it all the way through the material at each stroke. In and out, carefully and slowly.

"A cold perspiration broke out on the man looking at that strange apparition. His heart was beating so loudly that he thought surely this creature, if it were human and could hear, must hear him. But she did not move, so intent was she on her sewing. He stood it as long as he could. He could feel himself growing old, his hair turning gray and his skin wrinkling up into parchment. He would be an old man when he got out of this.

"But how to get out of it? Slowly he started to slide out of the opposite side of the bed, inch by inch so that he could be as quiet as possible. When finally he had slid out of bed he bolted out of the door, not looking back. He didn't know where he was going; all he wanted to do was to get away from that thing on the bed.

"On the steps he bumped into a man. With a groan of relief he recognized his English friend who had just come home. He felt just a little foolish, and decided not to tell his friend of his dream, because now, in the light, and with a friend, he felt sure that he must have been dreaming.

"The Englishman was hungry, and asked his friend to come down into the kitchen with him for a snack. The servants were in bed, and they could get themselves a little lunch. It was dark in the kitchen when they got there. The Englishman stumbled over something. Our friend, just behind him, slipped on something sticky, and the two of them almost collided. They switched on a light." Dick let his imagination run wild for the finish.

"On the floor, in a pool of blood, lay the headless body of the cook. The strange figure upstairs was real. It was a servant, gone suddenly insane, who had conceived a grievance against the cook, and had beheaded her with a butcher knife. She had taken the head upstairs with her and was pulling out the hairs, one by one."

When Dick finished this story there wasn't a sound in the room. Jo was pale and white. She looked around her in a frightened way. She was about to speak when there was a loud crash outside, as though a heavy body had been flung against one of the cabin walls. Jo screamed. Dick, himself a little white, jumped up. He ran to the door. There was nobody to be seen. He walked around the house. At one of the windows the snow was trampled down, as though somebody had been standing there looking in the window. The footsteps led off into the woods.

When Dick got back into the cabin, Jo looked at him wide-eyed. "What-what was it?"

"Nothing, I guess," said Dick. He did not want to tell Jo of his discovery that they had been watched. "It must have been snow falling off the roof."

"Oh," said Jo, "let's get out of here. It's almost stopped snowing, hasn't it, and the wind's gone down. They'll be worried about us if we stay much longer, and I don't like this place."

Silently they put on their wraps, strapped on their snowshoes and started the trek back. Once out into the air and away from the cottage, they recovered their spirits.

Dick said, "That was a pretty good story, wasn't it?"

"Oh, it was dreadful," said Jo. "I don't want to hear any more. And I think you were horrid to tell it."

"You really don't think I'm horrid, do you?" asked Dick, laughing.

Jo looked at him. She really didn't. And she might as well say so. "Well, I did think you were horrid, but when you saved me from death in the snow, I decided that you were pretty nice."

"Let's shake on that," said Dick, and they did, walking happily on through the snow.

They did not look behind them to see a sinister figure come out of the woods, stand at the door of the cabin and follow them malevolently with his eyes until they were out of sight.

The storm had stopped by the time they got home. "Come on in, we'll tell Pat about our cabin in the woods," said Jo. "And you can ask Yamoto then to help you drag in the tree tomorrow."

Dick Prentiss walked up to the porch of the lodge with her, but they hadn't begun to ascend the steps when the door was flung open and Mrs. Gruber, weeping loudly, came to meet them.

"Oh, dear, she's lost in the woods. I told her not to go out. She'll freeze to death!"

Dick ran up the steps. "What happened?"

"Miss Pat. She's gone into the woods alone, and been caught in the storm. She'll get lost, and we'll never find her. She'll freeze to death, and Mr. Duer will be so angry."

"Where did she go? Where's Yamoto?"

"He's gone. He's never around when he's needed. Oh, go find her, Mr. Dick. She'll be frozen."

"Come on," called Jo. "Come on, Dick. Don't stand around doing nothing. We've got to find her."

The two of them forgot their fatigue and turned about to enter the woods once more. "She's probably entered the woods by the path here. Leave it to you two to get into mischief."

But Jo said nothing. Her lips were set and her eyes showed the misery they felt. "You don't suppose anything's happened to her, do you?" she asked finally.

"No, of course not," said Dick. "We'll find her. She probably found some place to stay during the storm. Don't worry, Jo. You're still a twin."

And the two of them set off determinedly into the woods, calling and crying out as they went.

CHAPTER 8

Face to Face with the Mystery

WELTON DUER was experiencing a variety of emotions by the time he reached his cabin in the woods, got the door open and deposited Pat Faraday on his cot. The foremost was annoyance. Everybody had gone back on him. If Yamoto and Mrs. Gruber had followed his instructions, if this infernal girl had known enough to do as she was told, and hadn't been scatter-brained enough to walk into a snowstorm, he wouldn't have her on his hands now, half-frozen and unconscious. Now he was in for it! Even if he hadn't admitted it before, he had almost made up his mind that afternoon to go back to the Lodge. He was lonesome out here and uncomfortable. He thought with longing of being once more ensconced in his warm library, carefully coddled and pampered by his servants. But now going back was out of the question. Whereas before he might have arrived casually on the scene and pretended that he had returned from his business trip, now he had been found in his lair, and the explanations of why he was there would be too painful to make. He'd have to lie to this girl somehow and not let her know who he was. He knew that she'd never seen any pictures of him. What would he tell her?

Anxiety then for a moment overruled his annoyance. What was he going to do with her? He looked helplessly at the limp figure on the bed. If she had been a native workman overcome by sunstroke, or crushed by falling debris, he would have been all efficiency, and rendered first aid in a calm, cool manner. He thought of that calm, cool manner as he looked at the girl on the bed, and wondered why his fingers were so clumsy as he gingerly pulled off her cap and clumsily jerked off her sodden boots and jacket.

His next emotion was curiosity. This was, after all, the first time that he had seen this girl with whom his life was so intimately and yet so impersonally connected. She was pretty, he guessed. Looked athletic. She'd stuck out her harrowing experience in the woods without losing her head—that is, too much. If she'd had the sense she was born with, she'd never have gone into the woods anyway. What on earth had she been after? Her eyes were still closed. She was moving restlessly, though. Duer piled blankets on her and rubbed her arms and hands. They weren't frozen, but he ought to get the blood circulating. Lucky she'd been dressed warm enough. Ought to get something hot into her, too.

He fumbled clumsily among the cans of provisions

in the cupboard until he found some soup, opened the can, and put it into a saucepan on the little oil stove. When she came to, he'd feed her some of that. He glanced anxiously over at her from time to time. There was another emotion present that he could not place, indeed, that he would not have admitted even had he been able to place it. He only knew that he wanted to get her well enough to return her to her friends, and then give Yamoto and Mrs. Gruber what-for so that they would keep her in her place and not let her come bothering him again.

When Welton Duer turned from the stove, he stumbled over something. He looked down at the chest. Lord! He'd have to get that out of the way. Hastily he pushed it over to the door of the provision cupboard, and shut it up inside in the large space reserved for storing vegetables. He mopped his brow. What a mess this was. How was a man to get anything accomplished when he had to use so much energy in these little deceits? But that's what always happened when women came on the scene. They complicated things and brought confusion with them. A man couldn't accomplish anything with women around. He'd always known that. If she'd seen the chest he would have been lost. He knew now that he'd been right in not staying at the Lodge while these females were there.

But he looked across again at the female, and saw her scarlet cheeks and the damp curls that still held crystals of melting snow, and he somehow couldn't feel entirely annoyed. There was that other feeling that kept cropping up. He wished she would open her eyes. Maybe it wasn't warm enough in here. He bent over the fire and stirred it up, throwing enough wood on it to choke it almost completely. It was while he was bent over the fire that Pat opened her eyes and saw him. Then she looked down and saw the strange blankets that covered her, and her jacket and cap in a wet mass on the floor, and her eyes opened wide in bewilderment.

How had she got here? Who was that poking wildly at the fire? Whoever it was turned around and Pat quickly snapped her eyes shut. That would give her time to think. Anyway, it was pleasant to shut her eyes again. She was deliciously drowsy, and a tingling warmth was spreading over her body. Her brain was warm and drowsy, too, and she couldn't bring herself to attack the problem before her. She could hear the man walking toward her, now he was almost at the side of her bed. She must keep her eyes closed, and not let them twitch underneath their lids. Just before he reached her, he stepped on something and made unintelligible noises. Then he stopped and walked away. He was pulling a chair up to the fire. Pat concluded that he was hanging up her jacket. Well, at least she had another moment to think.

She gave her brain a little shake. Of course. This was the man who had found her in the woods. But who

was he? Suddenly she realized. The dismal railroad
station flashed before her, and its scabrous walls, and
the picture on those walls of the escaped convict. Mrs.
Gruber had warned her, Yamoto had warned her, that
if she went into the woods she would meet him. And
now she had. And what was she going to do about it?
She clenched her hands about the bedclothes in terror.
What would he do with her? He was probably furious
at her having found him in this hideout. A man who
would commit one crime would commit any number of
others to cover it up. He was coming toward her again.
Pat couldn't stand that. She sat bolt upright in bed,
clutching the clothes around her desperately.

Welton Duer gasped and dropped a cup of hot soup.
What in goodness' name had happened to the girl? She'd
jumped up out of a state of unconsciousness like a jack-
in-the-box, and now was absolutely wide awake and
normal, and staring at him as though he was about to
murder her. Annoyance was his uppermost emotion
now. It even blotted out that strange feeling that those
staring brown eyes gave him, and the realization that
he had wanted her to open those eyes so that he could
see whether they would be as he supposed they would.
The eyes were all that could be expected—but he was
annoyed. Some of the hot soup had splashed upon his
legs, and he felt that he looked an awful fool, standing
there in a puddle of soup. And why did she have to

keep staring like that, as though he were some strange animal?

For a long moment Pat continued to stare. She took in the tall figure before her, his amazed, yes, his scared expression, and then relaxed just a little. She knew instinctively that she was in no immediate danger. He did not look vicious—indeed, she would have said that he looked almost gentle—and certainly not like a desperate criminal. So she said, "You don't look like one, anyway."

Duer gasped at this amazing bit of information. He had certainly not expected these to be her first words. And he answered with an obvious question, "I don't look like one—what?"

Pat looked at him critically. "You've shaved."

Automatically, the man ran his hand over his chin and cheek. Yes, he'd shaved, but what did that have to do with it? "What don't I look like?" he persisted. What an asinine conversation to be having with this girl! He, a grown man. Well, he'd soon put an end to it and get rid of her. It irked him that she should be leading him on into this naive dialogue. It was that disarming manner of hers—

"You don't look like a convict," said Pat.

"A-a-convict?"

"I'm sorry. Perhaps you don't like to discuss it," replied the girl. "You know, we saw your picture at the railroad station. And Yamoto and Mrs. Gruber—those are the servants at Mr. Duer's house—warned me that I wasn't to go into the woods, for fear I'd meet you. But now I've met you—and you're not so bad." She sat back against the wall of the cabin and watched the effect of her disclosure on him. She might as well, she thought, lay her cards on the table, and let him know that she recognized him. It would force his hand, and let her know just where she stood.

If Welton Duer had not stooped down to cover his expression and pick up the pieces of broken china on the floor, Pat would have seen a strange reaction to her revelation. Because Welton Duer looked not startled, horrified, or chagrined at her disclosure, but relieved. So she thought that he was an escaped convict hiding in the woods. His problem of getting out of this situation was solved. He would play the part of the gentleman convict, and not have to disclose his real identity to her.

"You don't like to talk about it," repeated the girl.

Duer straightened up and stared piercingly at her. "No, I don't."

"Oh, I'm sorry. You probably don't want me here, either."

"Frankly, I'm not very much pleased. Your friends will be here looking for you, and then where will I be? I don't hide here to entertain you and your friends, you know."

Pat bridled. "After all," she said haughtily, "you brought me here. You needn't have, you know. Why did you rescue me at all? You could have just left me out there in the woods."

Welton Duer looked hurt. "I suppose that would be the way a convict would act, wouldn't it? You really couldn't expect much more from him. Once a man has committed a crime, he loses all self-respect, all common decency."

"I'm sorry. Sorry again," said Pat quietly. "I just wanted to impress on you the fact that I didn't barge in on you here. I was brought here, and by you. And you needn't worry that my friends will be here to get me. Nobody knows where I am."

Duer looked annoyed. "If you'd been doing as you should, you wouldn't be in this situation, young lady. What were you doing in the woods alone? These woods are no place for a child like you." He walked over to the fuel-box and threw the broken pieces of china into it so roughly that the fragments shattered as they fell.

Pat bristled. "Well," she said, "I shan't bother you any longer. If I may have my things—" She pushed off the blankets and got out of bed. The first step was disastrous. Her knees wouldn't hold her, and she stumbled forward. Welton Duer caught her.

"Get back into that bed," he snapped. Pat lay back meekly. She felt just a little giddy, and the bed was so comfortable. "Now you stay there until you get some of this food into you. And don't try any of those tricks again."

"Well," said Pat, regarding him coldly, "I'm not a child. And I've been told I wasn't welcome here."

Duer had filled another cup with soup, and brought it over to the bedside. "You're here, and I've got to make the best of it. Drink this."

Pat took the cup with shaking hand.

"Think you can manage it?"

"I think so," said the girl. Slowly she drank the hot soup. Duer sat over at the other side of the cabin, looking unconcerned, and wondering how well his pose of convict was working. He also wondered how he was going to get her back to the Lodge without anyone's seeing them. And most important of all, he wondered if he could persuade this child that she must tell no one that she had seen him there. He thought only too late that if he were an escaped convict, the girl was duty bound to turn him over to the police. He was too deeply in this thing to be exposed now. His one motive in life was not to be discovered as a coward and liar for he admitted that he was being both of these things by Pat and Jo. He watched the girl on the bed out of the corner of his eye. She looked fresh and simple and honest, certainly not the kind who would take kindly to one who had been deceiving her. He must keep up his deception at all costs. All hopes of ever getting back to the Lodge and comfort vanished.

The girl was talking to him. "You know, you're not a bad sort. Rather cross, but not bad."

He did not answer. There did not seem to be a need for any answer.

"That probably comes from living alone," Pat went on.

Welton Duer whirled around. "What?"

Pat almost dropped her cup. "Oh, what I mean is, well, you don't have much company here, do you?"

Duer was relieved. For just a moment he had been worried, thinking that the girl knew more than she should. But now he was assured that it had just been a random shot.

There was another silence. Duer poked up the fire. Pat watched the rather graceful movement of his hands. "Would you mind very much," she asked finally, shyly, "if I asked you why you are a convict? That is, what crime have you committed?"

The man looked into the fire. "I didn't commit any crime," he told her.

Pat's eyes widened. "You—didn't commit any crime? Then why were you—arrested and sent to prison?"

For a moment he did not answer, then he said, "I was shielding someone else. I was covering up the foolishness of another man. A fine man, a good man but not exactly responsible for everything that he did. One of these irresponsible acts caused a great deal of trouble. There were many complications, and I was forced to cover up this act. That is how I became a convict." To himself he said, "that is indeed how I became one." He was rather proud of the fact that by quick thinking and cleverly phrasing his half-truths he had been able to answer the girl's question and still keep his face. In fact, he was beginning to enjoy the situation. It was not at all hard to talk to this girl. In fact, it was rather pleasant. He hated to admit it, but still he stretched himself comfortably in his chair and took out his pipe.

Pat looked at him admiringly. "I think that that was wonderful," she said. "It was marvelous of you to do that. But why didn't he come forward and admit what he had done and save you?"

"He would never admit what he had done. Never. He would have lost face if he had, and that he would never do."

Pat bit her lip. "I think he was horrible," she said.

"On the contrary, young lady," said Welton Duer, puffing on his pipe, "he is a very fine man, and I think that you would have liked him. I hold no grudge against him—though he made me a convict."

"I'd hate him," said Pat decidedly.

Duer stared into the fire.

"What are you going to do now?" asked Pat. "You can't stay here all the time, can you?"

"I can stay here until the time is right. Then I shall try to get home."

"Home? Do you have a family?"

"No, not a family. But I have a home. I shall try to get back there someday."

"What if you are caught?"

Duer turned deliberately and regarded the girl steadily. "That depends a great deal upon you," he said at last.

"Upon me?"

"Upon you. Upon whether or not you give away my secret. Nobody will find me here. This section of the woods is not much frequented in winter. But, of course, perhaps you will consider it your duty to report me."

Pat's chin quivered. "I'm not that sort," she said slowly. "After all, you saved my life. You did, you know. And I like you."

Duer felt like a cad. Here he was working on the emotions of this sympathetic girl, and getting her to promise not to betray him, when he was betraying her. Well, it was her fault, really, for getting him into this situation.

"You shouldn't," said Duer. "I'm not a very admirable character."

Pat regarded him seriously. "But you are. In spite of the crossness. And the crossness is probably the result of being alone so much. You probably haven't had any women to take care of you. Will there be any women there—when you get home?"

The man did not look at her. "They'll be—gone," he said.

"Oh!" Pat's eyes were full of sympathy. No wonder he was bitter. He had been deserted when he went to prison. "All women aren't disloyal," she said.

"Perhaps not all. But most of them." This was Duer's heart-felt conviction, and he wondered why now he said it in such a half-hearted tone. Was it because he didn't want to hurt this girl? After all, why should he be so considerate of her. He'd known her such a short time— he'd never see her again. How stangely he was acting. It was as though another man were standing there in his place and saying these things. Well, after all, he was another man standing there. It was all very confusing.

His statement made Pat furious. She was all loyalty to her sex. "I think you're wrong," she said, her face slightly flushed with anger. "We're not almost all disloyal. You must not judge all women by the few you've met. Women have as much loyalty as men. I've never been let down by any girl I've ever known."

"I have," said Duer quietly.

"Oh." Pat's anger subsided. "I see then why you're so sour on all of us." Then she added impulsively, "I wish I could prove to you that we're not all deceitful. If I proved that to you would it make you feel differently toward things? Would you change your mind about the world and about women?"

Welton Duer had never, he told himself, seen anyone so fine and sincere and eager as that brown-eyed girl sitting up on his bed. If anyone could convince him that women were good and loyal, it would be she. So he replied, "If you will keep my secret for me, I will have more faith in human nature, and in the nature of women in particular, than I have ever had before."

The girl's chin stiffened. "I've given you my word," she told him, "and I'm going to keep it. I don't believe that you've done anything wrong. I trust you and believe your story. You must trust me and believe mine."

Welton Duer stood up and kicked at the fire. He threw a piece of wood on the waning fire and watched it blaze up. Then he turned deliberately to Pat, who had watched him closely during this process. She knew that he was stalling for time. She was surprised, though, by the expression on his face as he turned around and said, "I think that I do trust you." He looked like a changed man. For the first time she saw the dreamy mist soften the piercing gray of his eyes, and she liked the effect. Her intuition had been correct, she felt.

"Thank you," she said. She lay back on the pillow and drew the blankets closer around her. Her strength was fast returning to her. She felt that soon she would be able to get dressed and leave for home. But somehow she hated the idea. It was so pleasant being here and talking to this strange convict.

Duer had walked over to the window. "It's not snowing," he said. "Won't your friends be worried about you?"

"Oh, no doubt," answered Pat.

"How did you happen to come out alone, anyhow? What were you after?" went on the man.

For the first time since the moment when she had realized that she was lost in the woods, Pat remembered Welton Duer, and the chest that was to lead her to his whereabouts. Should she tell this man whose name she didn't even know about her suspicions regarding her guardian? He had trusted her with his secret, she could trust him with hers. "It's a long story," she said. "I was looking for a man. That is, I was looking for a chest."

Duer raised his eyebrows in startled surprise.

Pat thought that he did not understand her puzzling statements, so she went on to explain from the beginning. "You see," she said, "I was looking for Welton Duer. He's my guardian. If I found the chest, I'd be on the trail of the man."

Welton Duer sat down suddenly on a chair. He stared at the girl until she became uncomfortable, and hastened to tell her story, talking very fast, so that the words tumbled over each other. She told him about Welton Duer, and his friendship with her father, and his re-

lationship to Jo and her. Then she told him of their
first invitation to visit him, and of his strange disappearance. "You see," she said, "I couldn't figure out
why he should invite us after so long a time if he didn't
want to see us, and why he should be gone before we
came. And with all these strange things happening, I
just decided that I was going to turn detective, and find
out what was at the bottom of it all. His disappearance
seemed perfectly natural to everybody else, but I have
a feeling—an intuition, maybe, that there is something
mysterious about it all. I'd give anything to know. You
see, Mr.—you see, I really want to see him. It would
mean a lot to me." She asked eagerly, "Does it seem
strange to you, or do you think I'm silly, too?"

The man said nothing.

Pat's face fell. "You think I'm just a foolish girl. I
had thought you would help me some way. You know
the woods, and all that. But of course, if you don't think
that there's any mystery, you can't very well help me."

Still the man was silent.

Pat tilted her head a little to one side and regarded
him solemnly. "You can understand how hard it's been
for Jo and me. We've never had anybody to call our
own. That is, just Father, and that was for such a short
time. It's very lonely not having anybody. You know
that. That's why I feel the way I do about him. I
wanted so much for him to see us. You see, if he saw

us, I think maybe he'd like us, and want to see us often. Then we'd have somebody again. It would be like those old days with Father."

Welton Duer hitched his chair closer to the fire. He was not looking at Pat. "What sort of man is he?" he asked.

"Oh, I really don't know," said Pat. "We've imagined him as all sorts of things, Jo and I. We always thought of him as an old bear. That's because he hasn't liked us, and was so distant."

"He hasn't been so cruel to you. You've really had everything you wanted." Was Duer defending the man?

"Money, yes," said Pat. "But after all, that wasn't all that we wanted, or needed. We wanted to belong to somebody. To know that somebody would like to see the new clothes that we bought with our money, or be glad to hear that we were captain of hockey or baseball—that sort of thing. And Welton Duer was the person who could have done that. I'm sure that's what Father wanted him to do."

Duer stood up and paced nervously up and down the small cabin. "Maybe he wanted to," he said at last. "Maybe he wanted to, but couldn't. Perhaps he was a shy man—the queer sort who likes to be by himself. Maybe he was afraid that two girls would upset his well-planned life."

"Oh, but we wouldn't have. If he'd just given us a

chance we'd have proved that. All we needed was a chance. And now that we have our opportunity, this happened. No, I don't think that you can defend him that way."

But Duer went on defending the man, earnestly and sincerely, "I can understand him," he said. "Maybe I can't defend him, but I can understand him. He didn't want two women crashing down on him, and cleaning up the library that he loved because it was mussed up and home-like. He didn't want to feel saddled to one spot. From what you tell me of him, the world was his home, and he wanted to feel free to go where he pleased when he pleased. He may have had some emotional attachments that ended disastrously, and he wanted to protect himself from caring too much for anybody again. Oh, I can feel for this Duer person. I shouldn't be too hard on him, if I were you." He stopped talking, and leaned against the mantelpiece, his head in his hands.

Pat, surprised at the vehement outburst in defense of her guardian, regarded him curiously. She noticed the white, well-cared for hands, the beautifully shaped head—and suddenly the truth burst upon her. And as soon as it came to her, she felt that she had known it all along—had always known it. The man standing in the room with her was no convict. He was Welton Duer! Welton Duer was hiding out here in this cabin. Now everything became clear to her.

His mysterious disappearance; the warning not to enter the woods, so as not to discover him; Yamoto's trip into the woods with the chest that morning, the chest containing 'Mr. Duer's bones'—evidently fossil bones that were in some way connected with his work. That is, everything was clear except the motive. Why had this strange man deserted his comfortable home for the rigors of life in a log cabin, with only a small fireplace, old stove and lamps to heat and light it? What had happened to him between the time that he had sent the invitation to them, and the time that they arrived?

Thoughts were whirling through Pat's head at a great rate. She was glad that Welton Duer was not looking at her, so that she could recover her natural composure. Should she let him know that she had discovered him? She decided against that at once. There was some reason why he did not want her and Jo to know who he was, and until she found out that reason, she would never let him know. She had given her word not to betray him. But had it been her word not to betray Welton Duer? It had really been her word not to betray an unknown person, a convict. Did her word still hold?

Pat had never been in such a whirl in her life. Now she was really face to face with a mystery, the real mystery of Welton Duer. She looked at the man with entirely new eyes. So this was the man whom they had spent so much time describing to themselves, the man who had played such an important though anonymous part in the lives of the Faraday twins. Well, he was certainly mild enough. Nothing of the gruff old bear about this man. In fact, he looked quite chastened and crushed as he leaned against the fireplace. Pat felt a strange emotion well up within her. She was feeling sorry for this man. She wanted to comfort and mother him. How odd. Here was the person she and Jo had thought to depend upon for comfort and solace, and at their first meeting, he seemed to need solace himself. But she could do nothing, offer no comfort. Her one problem now was to get away from here so that she could plan a course of action. She had several thoughts on the subject, including a thorough and grim third degree for both Yamoto and Mrs. Gruber. Of the two, Mrs. Gruber seemed the most likely to succumb. That worthy with her pathetic grief would break down much more easily than the grinning Yamoto. The detective zeal in Pat kindled anew.

She felt a certain triumph, too. So Welton Duer had tried to make her believe that he was a convict, and had let her commit herself on any number of subjects. Well, now that she knew who he was, she would turn the tables. She would find out about him, without his ever knowing that she had discovered who he was. She smiled to herself at the thought. So women were stupid! Well, in this game, she was going to be cleverer than a

certain Mr. Duer. Just now she would let matters drop.
She'd get back to the lodge, and with the help of Jo,
Yamoto and Gruber, lay her groundwork, and with
facts in hand, confront the impudent guardian.

Aloud she said, "Let's forget Mr. Duer. I think that
I'd better be going. I feel quite well."

Duer, who had evidently forgotten that she was
there, turned in surprise at the sound of her voice, and
found her getting out of bed.

"Are my clothes dry?" she asked.

He went over and got them, and then walked over
to the other side of the room while she got into the dry
but stiffened garments.

"I'll see that you get back safely," he said. "I'll walk
back with you." He got into his own jacket and pulled
on his boots. "I can't go all the way, of course, but I'll
put you on the right path."

"That will be very nice," said Pat meekly. "I hate
to put you to any trouble."

"Not at all." They were both being horribly polite.

Pat still felt a little wobbly when they went out into
the cold air, but she soon braced up. Neither of them
noticed the small figure in black who slipped out from
behind a tree when they went off down the path.
Yamoto looked after them, grinning, then opened the
door of the cabin and went in. He might as well wait
where it was warm.

The man and girl made their way through the woods

in silence. Pat kept her eyes open for landmarks. "I'm coming back, you know," she said.

"You are?" Welton Duer raised his eyebrows. "Perhaps you had better not. Someone might follow you."

"I want to come back," said Pat. "I'll be careful to throw anyone off my trail when I come out. I think you need company. Being alone is bad for you."

"It's not so bad," said the man.

"Didn't you like my visit?"

"Yes, oh, yes. I did."

"Well, then, why can't I come again?" Pat smiled up at Duer with a very disarming smile.

"You may, if you wish." Welton Duer tried to sound casual but he wanted very much to see this girl again.

"I can't for a couple of days."

"Why not?" Was that disappointment in his voice?

"I'm going to the Prentiss' for a Christmas Eve party. We'll stay there all week-end. They're our neighbors, you know. They're having a week-end party. But I'll come out after that."

They stopped short. The sound of distant hallooing had reached each of them at the same moment. The sounds came closer.

"Your people from the lodge are coming after you," said Duer. "I'll leave you here. They mustn't see me. Goodbye. And thank you."

"Thank you," cried Pat, but the man was already crunching back along the path, and disappearing among the trees. "Until next time!" shouted Pat, but he did not look back. Then she began to halloo in answer to the shouts that were by now quite close. She ran forward a little, and then, in a small clearing, came upon Jo and Dick Prentiss.

"Pat!" cried her sister, and ran toward her. "You're all right! We were so worried. We waited until the storm was over before we went back to the lodge. You were gone, Yamoto was nowhere to be found, and Mrs. Gruber was in a state of hysteria. Are you sure you're all right? How did you get through the storm!"

"Oh, I found a shelter until the storm was over. I was quite warm and dry. You can see for yourself," laughed Pat.

"You shouldn't have come out," said Dick Prentiss, severely. But he couldn't stay severe long, because now that their anxiety was over, there was a general reaction, and a tendency to giggle. "Don't do it again," he ended weakly.

"Oh, I won't, sir," said Pat mockingly, "until the next time."

"But we were scared," said Jo. "We had visions of you all covered up with snow."

They walked back to the lodge, a happy chattering trio, full of Pat's miraculous escape, the splendid Christmas tree, and the costumes that they would wear.

When Welton Duer got back to his cabin after leaving Pat, he was much preoccupied. So he was startled when, on opening the door, he saw a small, black-clad figure sitting comfortably before the fire, smoking a cigarette. Yamoto was much preoccupied himself, dreaming his oriental dreams, and at first did not hear the door open. But when his master closed it behind him again with a slam, he jumped up and stood at attention, bowing little quick bows.

"Well, how did you get here?" asked Duer in surprise.

"I come in when you leave with young lady," explained the man.

Duer shot him a quick, suspicious look. "Where were you?"

"Oh, I all the time here," said the Japanese. "See, Boss, Yamoto see young lady go into woods. Then snow he come. And Yamoto go after young lady to see if she all light. I find she come here. I wait outside until you go. Then I come in."

At that moment Welton Duer decided that he loved his servant Yamoto. He had always known that the man was faithful, but this act of devotion touched him as no act undertaken for himself would have. "I'm getting soft and sentimental," he said. But just the same he began to make hazy plans for pensioning Yamoto, and providing for him in his old age. He noted that Yamoto had not been idle, either. There was a round moist spot on the floor where he had mopped up the spilled soup; the furniture was neatly rearranged; and from the stove came smells of a delicious lunch preparing.

"That was decent of you, Yamoto, to see that Miss Pat came to no harm." He thought also, how decent of Yamoto not to come crashing in when Pat was there, and give away his secret. Oriental tact, probably. And how discreet the man was being now! He went about the task of setting the table with his ordinary complacency, not mentioning a word about Pat's visit, or its effect on his master. Duer stretched out on the bed which had been freshly made up by Yamoto, and lighted his pipe. In just a little while the silence began to get on his nerves. He'd noticed before that when he was upset, the quiet movements which Yamoto made got on his nerves.

"Will you please rattle a few dishes, Yamoto?"

Yamoto grinned, raised his eyebrows, and obediently clattered a few dishes. He understood his master. Yet he did not say a word.

"Drat the man," thought Duer. "He's waiting for me to start the conversation. He wants me to mention Pat first. Well, he'll just have to wait."

The silence grew still more oppressive. Duer found himself wanting very much to talk about Pat. So he said suddenly, almost without his own volition, a sentence that he had been rehearsing to himself. "Well," he said, "I've seen your young lady."

"Yes," said Yamoto noncommittally. "Other one allee same."

"She's very nice. You've got good taste, Yamoto."

Yamoto dropped what he was doing and became voluble, "Oh, she nice. Velly nice. You likeum, huh? Other one nice, too. Allee same you come home now, huh? You likeum young ladies, you come home?"

Duer sat up very quickly. "No!" he said. "And not a word to the young ladies about me, either, do you hear?" Duer thought of cancelling Yamoto's pension, and then remembered that it hadn't yet been provided for. Just as well. The man took too much for granted. Because he didn't find Pat objectionable, Yamoto jumped to the conclusion that he had changed his mind about women and their deceitfulness. No, it would take more than the wiles of one youngster to bring about any change in him. Thus argued Welton Duer, in the same manner as a little boy would have whistled in passing a graveyard. He was keeping up his morale against a change that he felt taking place in him.

He got up and began to pace up and down, getting very much in Yamoto's way. Yamoto was taking biscuits out of the oven placed on top of the oil burners. "Almost ready, Yamoto?"

"Almost leady," said Yamoto, very much subdued. He had gone meekly back to his work after his master's outburst. These Americans! He might as well give up trying to understand them. They wanted one thing and did another; meant one thing and said another. "Dinnee almost leady."

Duer went to the window and looked out at the snow. He was thinking of Pat, and what she had told her friends when she met them. Would she be able to keep the secret of his being a convict from her sister? Great Scott! A convict. He had almost forgotten that. He was a convict. She was a brave little thing. He hadn't been able to scare her. She'd talked him down, all right. Well, she probably got that from her dad. He wondered what Jo was like. Yamoto said that they were both the same. But perhaps all western women looked the same to Yamoto, you couldn't tell.

Yamoto had to call him twice to lunch, but when he once started, he ate with appetite. He said no more to the servant, who quietly cleared up the cabin and left, promising to be back in time to prepare supper.

Yamoto was about half-way home when he met Dick Prentiss going out to Duer's cabin. Dick and he were old friends, and Dick, clever wretch that he was, could worm almost anything that he wished to know out of the otherwise taciturn Yamoto. Now the Japanese told Dick of Pat's visit to the cabin, and of Duer's refusal to give himself up, even now.

"We'll have to do something about this, eh, Yam? This has gone far enough. A man can be eccentric, but when he gets downright crazy, we've got to do something about it, don't we?"

Yamoto nodded and grinned. When he went on his way he felt that this clever young American boy would find a way. And Dick did.

He discovered his friend Duer with a book open before him, staring into space, and lit into him, without giving the man a chance to protect himself. He told him that he knew all, and that now Duer would have to come out into the open, admit his identity to Pat and Jo, and come back to the lodge.

"But I can't possibly, now," said Duer, when the boy finally stopped.

And Dick, who had expected just this, suddenly took a new tack. "Well, if you can't do that, at least you can act a little human. Come to our Christmas Eve party."

"—not possibly—" (Duer)

"—absolutely—" (Dick)

"—should say not—" (Duer)

"—must—" (Dick)

And Dick:

"I've got a plan, Welty. Now, keep quiet and listen to me. This is a grand plan. You can come to the party and no one will know who you are. You'll be absolutely incognito. Now isn't that better than being here by yourself on Christmas Eve? And you'll be able to see both of the twins, and our glorious Christmas tree, and so forth and so forth and so forth. The benefits are overwhelming. The drawbacks are negligible. The objections are non-existent."

But evidently some objections did exist, because it was half an hour before Duer would admit that the idea had any merit at all; it was an hour before he would say that he might consider it; and it was an hour and a half before he would accept unconditionally Dick Prentiss' plan to have him come to the Christmas Eve party as Santa Claus.

"Of course, Mother has arranged that Yamoto should dress up and ditsribute the gifts. But you can fix that with him. He'll love giving up the job. The suit never did fit him."

Dick was jubilant. On his way home he whistled and sang, and cut more than one caper as he thought of his clever scheme to get Welton Duer out of his shell and into human form. "Well done, well done, Dick, old boy," he said, capering.

CHAPTER 9

Pat Has a Plan

"How could you keep that from me for two whole days?" asked Jo of Pat. The secret that Pat had kept was that of Welton Duer's hiding place in the woods and her accidental visit to it.

"Well," said Pat. "In the first place, I promised him that I wouldn't tell anybody about him. That is, I promised that I wouldn't tell anybody about a convict who lived in a cabin out in the woods. Now, that's very different from telling you about Welton Duer's living out there, isn't it?" Pat looked anxiously at Jo. For two days she had been trying to decide whether she would tell her sister about her adventure or not. At last she decided that she just had to. And she did.

They were standing in front of the Prentiss' fireplace, eating sandwiches and drinking hot chocolate. They were full-fledged members of the house party now, and were enjoying themselves hugely. This afternoon of the Christmas Eve party, Mrs. Prentiss had shooed all her guests out-of-doors, skating, skiing, hiking, and she and Yamoto had trimmed the Christmas tree, which now stood almost concealed by a decorated screen in one corner of the room. The guests could come in when they chose, for dinner tonight was an informal affair, consisting of sandwiches and chocolate, which they might eat when they chose, before going up to dress for the party proper, which was to begin with the lighting of the tree.

Pat and Jo were almost the last to come in. Most of the early comers were already in their rooms, napping or dressing, and Pat had taken the opportunity of their being alone to tell Jo what had been on the tip of her tongue for so long.

"In the second place," she said, "I didn't know exactly what I was going to do about it. But I have a plan."

Jo opened her eyes wide, as she took a large bite of sandwich. "What are you going to do?"

"What are we going to do, you mean," her sister replied. "Because you're going to help me—that is, if you're game."

"If I'm game," said Jo contemptuously. "Do you think I'm not? Have I ever not been?"

"Oh, you might not want to do this," said Pat. "It really isn't quite bright. But it's the only plan I can think of now."

"Well, what is it?"

Pat put down her chocolate cup. "It's this," she said. "You and I are to leave the party tonight, and slip away to Welty Duer's cabin. We'll tell him that we know all, and make him come back with us to the party. How does that strike you?"

Jo looked disapproving. "Not so well," she said frankly. "He won't come."

"Oh, I don't know," replied Pat. "Anyway, we can try. I hate to think of him all alone out in that cabin on Christmas Eve. Just think how lonely he'll be, Jo. Come on, be a sport. You'll come with me, won't you?"

Jo smiled. "It's a hare-brained idea, but it's yours, so I'll see you through with it."

"Good egg," said Pat. "We'll leave about ten or so."

"If we can sneak away," Jo said.

Pat looked superior. "I've looked after all that. We can slip into our room here on the first floor, and out the door that leads to the porch, over the railing, and off to the woods. We'll have to wear our warm clothes, of course. That's just a detail."

"You're a marvel," said Jo. "But we'd better get dressed now. We'll never get down in time."

Jo turned, and almost ran into Mrs. Gruber, who was coming in with hot chocolate."

"Oh, Miss Jo," she cried, "you almost spilled all the hot chocolate. You do give a body a turn the way you throw yourself about, without warning. We both might have been scalded." She put down the pitcher she was carrying and made her complaining way out of the room.

"I wonder how much she heard?" asked Jo.

Pat laughed. "I think Gruber's so wrapped up in her own grief that she doesn't hear what other people have to say. Let's go up."

But their going was interrupted once more. The front door opened and Mavis Martin breezed in, her skates slung over her shoulders.

"Hi, twins," she called. "Wait up for Mavis. Have a sandwich with me for old time's sake."

"We're stuffed up," said Jo, but nevertheless, they came back to talk to her.

Mavis Martin was their favorite among the week-end guests, and to complete the pleasure, the twins were her favorite as well. The three had taken to each other immediately, and with Dick, they formed the gayest quartet in the house. Mavis was not young—that is, in years. She was about thirty. She had married early and become a young widow, a slim, dark-eyed, dark-haired, gypsy widow, who skated and ran and danced like a girl. In fact, the twins, athletic as they were, had a hard time keeping up with Mavis Martin. She was the center of the party—everything seemed to revolve about Mavis, who accepted any homage paid to her very naturally and unaffectedly, as though it were her due.

Pat watched the woman as she sat on the arm of a

chair and poured herself a cup of coffee. Her flushed cheeks, her black wind-blown hair made her look more like a gypsy than ever. At last Pat said:

"Mavis, if I were a man, I wouldn't rest until I'd married you."

Mavis laughed. "It's a good thing you're not a man, Pat, because I'd refuse you."

"You would," laughed Pat. "Why?"

Mavis became suddenly serious. "I'm never going to marry again," she said. "You know I was married once. And I found that if you marry some one you don't love, well, it's better not being married at all."

Jo asked: "But why did you marry him, if you didn't love him?"

Mavis shrugged her shoulders. "Oh, money, and social position, and that sort of thing. They seemed important at the time. And then it seemed important to show somebody how independent I was. And I discovered that I wasn't."

"Did he want to marry you, too?"

"Yes, but we quarreled. I forget about what. And I had to show him that I could marry anybody I cared to."

Jo and Pat were silent. Mavis broke the silence with a little laugh. "Listen to Auntie Martin telling you about her youthful romance and blighted love. Come, come, this will never do. We've got to be in a festive mood tonight. Only a last word—if you aren't in love with somebody, don't marry him, no matter what; but if you are, well, marry him—no matter what."

With a final laugh, Mavis ran up the steps. "You young ones had better get dressed," she called down from the top and disappeared.

The twins went into their room, where their costumes were laid out on the bed. They hadn't counted on a masquerade when they had packed, but had managed, by ransacking their wardrobes, to make up outfits that were more than presentable. They were going to come to the party as Italian troubadors, their costumes consisting of the long and voluminous black velvet trousers from their lounging pajamas, red silk scarves about the waists, the white silk blouses that they ordinarily wore with their dress suits, and jaunty silk bandanas about their hair, made from two large and decorative handkerchiefs kindly lent to them by Dick Prentiss.

"How do I look?" asked Pat, in front of the mirror, where she had just finished tying her bandana to suit her.

"Grand," said Jo. "Here give me a hand with this." Pat went over to her and deftly tied her sister's bandana so that it looked just like hers.

"Do you think they'll recognize us?" she laughed.

"They'll recognize you, but not me," said Jo with a mischievous grin. "Does it make any difference, any-

their masks, and, still laughing, they went out into the gayly lighted room. Everyone turned to see them enter. They did make a beautiful picture, these two slim lovely girls in their boyish costumes.

"Welcome, Youth," cried out Tommy Hastings, who looked mountainous in his clown suit of red and yellow. He rushed up to them, and taking each by the hand, brought them down to the center of the room.

How gorgeous everybody looked. That gay cavalier, that must be Mr. Houghton; and the gypsy with loads and loads of glittering jewels, that was Mavis Martin. And the Mandarin and the Chinese lady, Dr. Gordon and his wife. And that tramp—that hideous tramp with a missing tooth—why, that was the scamp, Dick Prentiss. He would make himself look as horrible as possible! And old Mr. Henry even had conceded to the spirit of fun, and was wearing a funny sort of little hat on his white hair.

Pat and Jo didn't feel a bit frightened now. Everybody was so gay and jolly.

"Hi, gay troubadors," cried Mavis. "Make music for me."

Obediently Jo sidled up to her, dropped on one knee, twanged an imaginary guitar, and with languishing sighs, sang to her a gypsy love song.

"Beautifully sung, my hero," cried Mavis, amid the applause.

"Beautifully done," said Mrs. Prentiss, coming up to

her. Mrs. Prentiss, elegant in a blue velvet hostess gown, had been counting noses, and had discovered that all of her chicks had gathered round. She turned to them. "I think that we shall light the Christmas tree now." After a little coaxing and fluttering she had them grouped about in front of the screen. At a signal from her, Yamoto turned out the lights. They hadn't realized how dark it had grown, until they were plunged into blackness. Then the lights of the tree were thrown on. Up sprang a myriad of green, red and blue dots of light, shining on the tinsel, picking up the highlights of the golden and crimson balls that hung in profusion all over the tree, the silver stars, the silver icicles, and the glittering snow. It was a beautiful tree, and Yamoto had done himself proud. He hovered now, like a good fairy who has changed a pumpkin into a coach and is pleased with the effect.

"O-o-o-h." This from the guests, that is, the feminine guests. The masculine ones admired in masculine silence. Pat swallowed hard. It was one of the most beautiful things she had ever seen.

Then suddenly, when the tree had been enough admired, the lights went up again, and the radio, turned on by Dick, blared out some gay dance music. The solemn ceremonies were over; the party proper was beginning.

Tommy swooped down upon Jo, and whirled her away. Thus began her first really grown-up party. Dick, knowing that he looked wretched when he grinned, ambled up to Pat and claimed the first dance as his.

"You do look awful," said Pat, as they glided away.

"Do I?" muttered Dick, and then grinned some more.

"You do," said Pat.

Dick became suddenly serious. "Then I shouldn't be dancing with you. Because you look beautiful."

"Do I?" laughed Pat.

"You do," said Dick softly.

They danced in silence for a few moments. Then Dick said, "You dance divinely. What tough luck, my having to go back to college just when I've met you."

"Do you think so?" whispered Pat, inwardly laughing. She knew that Dick Prentiss wasn't so heartbroken about losing her, Pat. The poor boy thought that he was dancing with Jo. Evidently Jo had promised him the first dance, and had been carried off by Tommy before she had a chance to dance with him.

"It was such good luck, though, my meeting you. I shouldn't complain."

"No, you shouldn't," said Pat. Then she added. "That's certainly a sweet thing for you to say. And Jo said that you never said sweet things."

"What!" said the tramp, looking down closely at the troubador.

"Jo says that you never said sweet things to her."

Dick Prentiss recovered his poise, and stopped stepping on Pat's toes. He said nothing, but danced very stolidly and silently after that.

"That's Jo, dancing over there with Tommy," said Pat.

Dick danced over to them. "I'm going to cut in on Tommy," he said. "You don't mind, do you, Pat?"

Pat laughed. "Oh, of course not. But what a waste of time. Poor Dick. You'll have to start all over again. You know how it starts, 'You're looking so beautiful—' "

"You keep that to yourself," warned Dick and made a terrible face at Pat. "Don't ever let me hear that you've told anybody what's happened here tonight."

Pat promised. The Doctor, who had not taken part in the dancing, came over and tapped Dick on the shoulder. "You can't dance with her all evening," he said, and took Pat away in a sedate embrace. Dick cut in on Jo, leaving Tommy for the moment without a partner, which condition he remedied by swooping down on the Doctor and Pat, and whirling the girl away with him.

"You know, I thought it was you I was dancing with all the time," he said earnestly in her ear.

Pat laughed. "Oh, Tommy, you clown. You don't need a costume to make you funny."

Tommy looked at her ruefully. "That doesn't sound like much of a compliment," he said.

Pat squeezed his hand. "It is a compliment. You're an old dear, Tommy."

Tommy had to be content with this, for they were cut in on at this point by the gay cavalier, and separated.

The party progressed gayly, in fact, so gayly, that the twins almost forgot their mission that night, and the clock crept to ten-thirty and past, before Jo became aware of how time had flown. She sought out her sister.

"Isn't it time to leave?" she whispered to her. The rest of the party had taken time out for charades, and were watching Tommy and Dick trying to convey to them the word "alligator," with much realistic wriggling and gaping, so that the two girls could withdraw without being missed. "Do you think that we can get away without being seen?"

"If we go now, I think that we can make it. Everybody is taken up with Tommy and Dick. Come on, quickly."

They made the bedroom door without being seen, and bundled up in the coats and boots that they had laid out ready to be used.

"Are you sure you know the way?" asked Jo, as they let themselves out the back door.

"Positive," said Pat. "I went over the path from here yesterday when you and Dick went skating."

Jo looked contrite. "You could have gone with us, you know. We asked you."

"Donkey," Pat said. "I didn't want to go with you. I wanted to be alone to see if I'd be able to find the cabin tonight. Oh, darling, look at that moon. It's just for us. Here, we go into the woods right about here. No, no there, but down there by that crooked pine. The one that looks like a little old man in the moonlight. Oh, Jo, isn't this glorious?"

"It's—it's wonderful," breathed Jo. "I've never seen anything so beautiful."

The air was still, and the snow crunched underfoot as they went into the silvered woods. The adventure before them seemed exciting and marvelous. That it was reckless and foolhardy, and not a little dangerous, never occurred to them. They clasped each other's hands, and almost in a dream went forward into the enchanted forest.

CHAPTER 10

Mavis Martin Proposes

WHEN the twins went out the back door, Santa Claus came in at the front. Yamoto let him in, with much wide grinning.

This Santa Claus burst surprisingly upon the guests. They hadn't expected a visit from the old fellow, isolated as they were up here in the Michigan woods, and even if they had expected him, his appearance would have been surprising. He was the leanest, and most disgruntled-looking Santa Claus in captivity.

Welton Duer wondered more and more as the seconds ticked by and the members of the house party became more and more hysterical with laughter, why he had ever let Dick Prentiss talk him into playing this asinine role. Of course nobody here recognized him in this costume, but still, he felt like a fool, and certainly he looked like one. This Santa Claus did not shake like a bowlful of jelly. He surveyed the crowd sourly and opened the pack he carried with him. Dick had arranged the presents, and each one was appropriate to the person to whom it was addressed. Dick had even got permission from Welton Duer to present Pat with the mummified head that had given her such a bad night when she and Jo first arrived at Duer's lodge.

Santa reached down into the bag, and pulled up the first package. It was for Dr. Gordon, and contained a jig-saw. Santa looked glumly at the party as they laughed at the doctor and his gift. He wished that he were back in the woods in his snug cabin. He thought with longing of how lonesome he would have been alone. Oh, blessed lonesomeness. At least he wouldn't have had on a too-warm red suit, and the most uncomfortable white whiskers in the world, not to mention the hot cap and ticklish wig that were pulled down over his ears. Santa looked at Dick Prentiss, who grinned back at him, in a black-toothed grin. Really, it was only by a miracle that Dick Prentiss got any gift that Christmas. Santa did not love him.

Santa Claus reached again into his bag. The gift was for Pat and Jo Faraday. He looked eagerly about, but nobody advanced for the package. Then everybody looked around. The twins were missed. Mrs. Prentiss turned to Yamoto, who was standing by, watching the festivities, and seeing that all was well.

"Yamoto," she said, "will you please call Miss Pat and Miss Jo?" As Yamoto left the room, she gave her attention again to her guests.

Santa drew out package after package. Finally there was only one left. He reached down and pulled it out. He looked at the card attached. Then a queer thing happened. Santa turned very pale. He looked once more at the card, and then around the crowd.

"Will—will Mavis Martin please come forward?" he asked. Mavis tripped up to him and curtsied. Santa stared at her with embarrassing scrutiny. The girl held out her hand and said:

"May I have my present, please, Mr. Santa Claus?"

Santa, still staring at her, withdrew his hand so that she could not quite reach the package. Then he said, strangely:

"I would rather give Mavis Martin her gift when we are alone."

Mrs. Prentiss, who had been counting noses again, could not figure out who this odd Santa Claus could be. Dr. Gordon was here, so was Mr. Henry—oh, dear, what worrisome guests she had. But she said:

"Mavis, why don't you and Santa Claus go into the library? There's a fire in there." How ridiculous that sounded, she thought to herself as she said it.

As the two walked toward the library, a look of sudden recognition came into Mrs. Prentiss' eyes, and old memories flooded into her mind. She smiled ever so slightly. Then very briskly she turned again to her guests and worried them once more into jollity, like a hen scattering her chicks who hovered too close. The library door closed behind Mr. Duer and Mavis Martin.

Inside, they stood facing each other, Mavis with her brow wrinkled, a quizzical, amused expression playing over her face. Never had she seen such a Santa Claus. There was something dear and pathetic, and yes, something familiar about him. At last she said, "May I have my gift now, Santa?"

But instead of handing her the package, Santa said, "Will you take off your mask, Mavis? I want to see if you are still as beautiful as ever."

"Of course," said Mavis. Her hand trembled as she reached up to take off the mask. That voice! She could never mistake it. How odd that she had not recognized it before. But then, coming from behind those ridiculous whiskers! No wonder she had not known him the moment he spoke out there. The mask was off, and the girl looked up with gleaming eyes at the eager figure towering above her.

"As beautiful as ever," he said huskily.

"Please take off those awful whiskers, Welty," said Mavis, her voice divided between laughter and tears.

Welton Duer took them off. For a long moment they simply looked at each other. Then the man took her hand and led her over to the sofa in front of the fireplace, where they sat down.

"I've been missing you all these years," he said to her, "but I never realized how much until just this moment."

"I've missed you, too, Welty. So much. What a fool I was."

"Oh, no. It was my fault. It was my fault for letting you go."

She put a hand over his mouth to stop his words. "It was I, Welty. I was a spoiled, capricious child. I wanted to show my power over you. I told you that if you went on that expedition that was to be gone a year, I would never see you again. You know that's what happened."

"And I went anyway. I was stubborn."

"Oh, no. You went because you loved me. You wanted to be somebody, to do things before you married me. And you knew I loved you. You thought that I'd surely be waiting for you when you came back. But as soon as you'd left, I married Sonny Martin. Just to show you how independent I was. But I suffered for it, Welty, really I did. I suffered for it, loving you, and married to him."

"Don't talk about it—please, dear. It's all past."

"Yes, it's past." They were both silent, until Mavis said:

"Do you think that you could ever forgive me, Welty?"

"Forgive you, Mavis? Darling, you must forgive me. Forgive me all these years of bitter thoughts that I have held against you—against all women. When I didn't see you for so long, I forgot how good and sweet and pure you really are, and made my own image of you out of my bitterness. But now that is washed away. It is washed away by one sight of you. How could I be such a fool?"

Mavis stroked his hand. "Can't we wipe out all those years of bitterness with years of sweetness? Can't we start over again?"

Duer smiled a pained smile. "I'm old, Mavis. Look at these white hairs." He stroked his wig.

"Oh, you idiot. Take that off."

"It's rather thin underneath."

Mavis reached up and pulled off the wig. She smoothed down the hair that had become disarranged in the process. "Oh, not so old, Welton Duer."

"I'm more stubborn than ever. No woman could put up with me. I'm terribly crotchety before breakfast."

"I'd see that the breakfast was so good, you'd turn into a lamb just thinking about it."

"There are my expeditions. I come and go as I choose. I am away for years at a time."

"That's all right. I'd go with you."

"To Africa? Into the jungles? Mavis, no woman can stand it."

"I could. I'm strong, Welty. You've no idea how I've changed. I've made myself strong in mind and body. I'd go anywhere—with you."

Welton Duer shook his head. "I can't ask it of you. And there is another thing that I haven't mentioned to you. I am going to take on an added responsibility that I can't ask you to share."

Mavis bit her lip. "What is that?" she asked quietly.

"You have probably been with two charming girls for the past two days—the Faraday twins."

"Yes, I have," said Mavis. "They are darlings. How do you know them?"

"Don't you remember, Mavis? My wards? Faraday's girls?"

Mavis' eyes lighted with recollection. "Oh, of course. How could I have forgotten?"

"I have decided to adopt them. Make them my legal daughters."

"Welty! How wonderful."

Duer snorted. "Don't pin any medals on me, Mavis. Heaven knows it's late enough that I'm doing my duty. I've neglected them shamefully. I wouldn't even see them. I was afraid of them. You made me afraid of women, dear. I was afraid that they'd grow up and be deceitful and mean."

Mavis bowed her head. "I'm sorry I did that to you."

"Oh, I was probably born crotchety, dear. But it was too bad for those poor children. Because I worried about what they would do to me when they grew up, I neglected them all their lives, let them grow up among strangers, unloved and unwanted. And they're such lovable children, Mavis."

"Oh, they are. I know that. But Welty, I love them, too. Won't you let me help you—make it up to them? Won't you let me make brighter the lives that I darkened? It was really my fault that you neglected them. I want to dedicate the rest of my life to making up for that." Mavis' eyes were shining with tears.

Duer looked at her closely. "You really want to, my dear? You mean that? Think carefully, Mavis. It is a great responsibility. I want them to have every care, every loving kindness in the world."

"Trust me, Welty. I will be good to them. My life is empty now. I want to fill it with you and them. You don't know how lonely I've been. There have been parties and good times, yes, but when I'm alone, there are always memories. Help me, Welty, to stifle those memories. Let me have a present, so that the past will be blotted out. Let me work for you."

The man took her hands in his. "Don't plead like that, Mavis. I should be the one to plead for your help and forgiveness. I don't want you to sacrifice your life and youth for me. I'm not worth it. Really I'm not."

"I'll take that chance, Welty. I've never proposed to a man before. Welton, will you marry me?"

He bent down and kissed her on the forehead. At that moment the door burst open. Dick Prentiss at any other time would have been startled to see Santa Claus kissing Mavis Martin, but now he had more urgent thoughts to occupy him.

"The twins are gone!" he cried. "We can't find them anywhere. Mrs. Gruber is crying and wailing in there that she thinks they went into the woods. She heard them talking about it. Of all the fool things to do! At this time of night!"

Duer jumped up. "For heaven's sake! We've got to do something, Dick. We've got to go after them!"

"I'll go, too," said Mavis.

"You'd better stay, Mavis," said Dick. "We men will go."

"I'm going, too," she persisted.

The three of them rushed into the front room, where the confusion at the discovery of the twins' absence had reached its highest pitch.

CHAPTER 11

Trapped

Jo AND Pat were both glad and sorry when they saw the lights of Welton Duer's cabin shining out at them through the trees. They were glad, of course, to have found it at all. Their feet, even in their stout boots, were getting numb; the calmness of the night had been deceiving. They were sorry, because it meant that finally they were going to come face to face with their guardian, and now that the prospect was so near, they weren't so sure that they could carry it off.

"What do you suppose he'll say?" said Jo. "I know he'll be angry. He has every right to be."

"Oh, no, he won't," said Pat, reassuringly. After all, she had been the one who had actually seen the man, and she meant her words to carry weight. But she herself was beginning to feel a little doubtful as to the wisdom of coming here. After all, she had told Welton Duer that she wasn't going to tell anybody about him—or had she? There was that old question again. Would

182

she be able to convince him that she was acting honestly, or would he think that she was just evading the issue, and wriggling out of her dishonesty with the excuse that he had asked her not to tell anyone that he was a convict? Pat somehow began to wish that they had not come. It seemed such a good idea back at the Prentiss', but it seemed such a foolish idea now. In fact, no sort of idea at all.

They approached the cabin door.

"You knock," whispered Jo.

"You knock," whispered Pat.

In the end they both knocked together.

There was no answer. They knocked again. Still no answer. But there was a light in the window.

Evidently he wasn't asleep. Cautiously, Pat edged around until she was opposite the window, and peeped into the room. It was empty, but the brightly burning fire, the general atmosphere of the room suggested that someone had just stepped out for a moment, and would be right back.

"He's gone out," she relayed to Jo.

"Well," said Jo, her teeth chattering. "Let's go inside. That will be better than standing out here freezing to death. If he doesn't want us, he can put us out. But at least, we'll be warm."

They pushed on the door. It opened, and they entered the cabin. It seemed disordered and untidy, quite different from its appearance when Pat had last seen it.

"He's left his hat," said Pat. "Gracious, what a messy old thing it is!" She held off at arm's length a battered, greasy old hat that looked very ancient indeed. "I can't imagine him wearing that," she added. She tried to think of Welton Duer in this headgear, and couldn't.

Jo was looking about the room. "I should think he'd rather live at the lodge," she said, and sniffed. "Even if we were there."

Pat started to clear up the cluttered table. "Maybe we can get the dishes washed before he gets here. That might put him in a better humor. Come on, lazybones."

They put some water on the stove to heat, and proceeded to straighten up the room. The room was tidied, and no Welton Duer appeared. The dishes were washed, and still no Welton Duer. Pat began to fidget. Well, what next?

"Where on earth can he have got to?" asked Jo.

"Certainly not far. Where would he go? He wasn't a neighborly sort of person, so he hasn't gone calling."

Now that they had nothing to do, the atmosphere of the room began to oppress them. While they were busy they hadn't noticed so much how gloomy and silent it was out here. Now the woods seemed to close in about them, and hem them in, almost suffocating them. It wasn't a reassuring sort of feeling, either. They were all alone now. They wished Welton Duer would hurry up and come in if he were coming.

"What a place for a murder," said Jo, gloomily.

"Nobody would ever find you here—not for months, anyway."

Pat stared at her in horror. "Oh, Jo, please. Don't talk about such things."

"Well, what is there to talk about?"

They were silent for a long time. Then Pat said:

"I wish we hadn't come."

"So do I."

They heaved heartfelt sighs.

"But," added Jo, "now that we're here, we're here. We're going to see our guardian, and have it out with him. What a nuisance he is, getting us out here on Christmas Eve."

Pat smiled just a little. "Well, after all, whatever his sins, you can't blame him for that. It isn't really his fault that we're here. He'd probably be more pleased if we'd stayed at the party."

"Such a nice party," sighed Jo. "Whose idea was this to leave it?"

Pat looked penitent. "Mine," she said. "I'm sorry."

"That's all right," said Jo. "I was just as foolish to follow you out here."

"It would be all right if he'd only come!"

Then the thought struck both of them: had something happened to Welton Duer out in the woods? Was he lying hurt somewhere? He had certainly stepped out only a minute or so before they left, because he'd left the fire burning brightly.

"What shall we do?" asked Jo.

"Wait," said Pat.

They waited, sitting close together on the bed, holding tightly to each other's hands. Then Pat jumped up.

"Let's put the dishes away in the cupboard." She felt that she wanted to be busy. As she opened the door to the cupboard, her eyes lighted on the chest, which Duer had pushed in there to conceal from her.

"Oh, Jo, look. The chest."

Jo came over and together they stared down at it. They were both remembering the first time that they had seen it, and their horror that night when their loneliness had overcome them at the lodge, and they were caught in the grip of some unknown terror. Now as they looked at it, it seemed again to take on a sinister appearance. Once more it was the mystery chest, containing they knew not what horror.

"Oh, close the door, Pat. That thing gives me the shivers."

But Pat did not close the door. Instead, she swooped down and pulled out the chest, so that it stood in the center of the room. "I'm going to open it," she said with determination.

Jo looked horrified. "Oh, Pat, don't. It isn't ours, and if Mr. Duer should come in—"

"I'll get it open in a second. See? The top isn't locked now. He's left it open. All I have to do is raise it, and we'll have this thing settled once and for all. Here, help me lift it up."

"Well, if you must," said Jo. "Pat, I don't like this."

Together they kneeled down before the chest and prepared to lift the lid. Behind them the door creaked and pushed open. Without daring to turn around, Pat looked at Jo and Jo looked at Pat. They both blushed a fiery red. They had invaded Welton Duer's cabin, and had been caught in the act of pilfering his private property. What would he think of them now? All hope of ever convincing him that they were nice young women was gone. He'd hate them forever now.

He was standing just behind them now, not saying a word. Silently they both rose and turned around.

They found themselves facing the muzzle of a gun. Pat screamed. This wasn't Welton Duer at all. It was somebody else. Somebody, dirty, dishevilled, horrible to look at, had come in, and was covering them with a gun. The two girls almost fainted from fright. They stood there a terrible moment, their knees trembling.

"Well," growled the man. "What you doin' here?"

Neither Pat nor Jo could answer. Their mouths were dry, their tongues paralyzed. They knew now who this was, this tattered, bleary-eyed, whiskered creature before them. It was the convict whose escape had occasioned so much alarm. This was the man whom Pat had imagined Welton Duer to be.

"Well, why don't you say something?" He leered at them unpleasantly. "Pretty brace of young ones, ain't you? Hanged if I don't like company. Livin' like a lord today, and that's a fact. Fine food, fine house, and two ladies to keep me company. So the gentleman who lives here keeps you two to red up for him, does he? Nice convenient arrangement. Don't know that I don't like it myself."

He stuck his gun in his belt and walked toward them. Terrified, the two girls backed away as he advanced. He reached out a large, hairy hand and grasped Jo's arm. "Come over here, and let me see you," he said with a nasty laugh.

"You let her alone!" screamed Pat, and rushing at him, beat him with her fists.

Slowly the man turned to her, not releasing his grip on Jo's arm, and pushed her with such force that she went stumbling across the room, and collapsed on the cot. Jo screamed.

The man snorted. "Go on, scream. Who's going to hear you? The squirrels in the trees, maybe. I've been living with them for a long time. They're my pals, the squirrels. I've eaten a lot of my pals, too." He laughed again, that rasping, horrible laugh. Jo tried with all her might to pull her arm out of his grasp, but he clung with a grip of iron and drew her toward him.

Pat could not stand that. Like a fighting terrier, she jumped up, and rushed at the man once more. Together she and Jo beat at him, harrying him until he snarled like an animal. "Oh, so you're going to try that, are you? Well, you won't get away with it. I don't want to be bothered. When your gentleman friend comes back, he'll find you both pretty cold." In a rage, he shook them off and stepped back. His hand went toward the gun in his belt.

But he did not draw it out. The door behind him opened. He whirled about to see who was entering and saw Yamoto standing in the doorway. His face was pale above the black of his coat, and the black of his stiff hat. He was not grinning, but was deadly serious.

"Yamoto!" cried Pat. "Yamoto! He's got a gun!"

"Another one," snarled the convict. "Another weasel. Well, Chink, you might as well take it, too." He drew his gun from his belt and raised it to fire. There was a sudden pantherlike spring, and the gun hurtled across the room. Yamoto had knocked the gun from his hand.

While the convict was looking in surprise at his empty hand, Yamoto calmly took off his hat and coat. "We fight," he said.

The man threw back his head and laughed, "You? Why, you—" His voice changed to a growl of rage. "I'll break your neck with one hand."

Yamoto edged away. He seemed frightened. Off in one corner, Jo and Pat clung together. They did not like to watch. Poor Yamoto was going to sacrifice himself for them. They wanted to help, but there was nothing they could do. The men were between them and the gun. If they could only get to it. Trembling, they looked on.

The great man advanced upon the tiny one, his arms swinging, ready to lunge. Suddenly there was a scramble of arms and legs, and a great crash. The convict lay prone on the floor of the cabin, Yamoto standing over him. He had not counted on ju-jitsu, but Yamoto had. He threw himself upon the man on the floor. But the hulking creature threw him off and stood up unsteadily upon his feet. He swung a huge arm at the Japanese. If he had touched him, it would have meant a knockout blow to Yamoto, but he cleverly dodged, and since the convict had laid himself open to the attack, plunged at him again, and easily threw him over his back.

Pat laughed. It was an hysterical laugh, halfway between laughter and tears. But it did look so funny to see little Yamoto swinging that big brute about. Jo looked at her sister in amazement and then she, too, laughed, the tears running down her cheeks. They clung to each other and giggled. But suddenly they caught their breaths in a gasp.

The last fall had brought their enemy close to his own gun. His hand stretched out for it. Yamoto saw him, and tried to kick the gun out of the way. He was too late. The man's hand closed over it. He struggled to his feet, swaying drunkenly.

"I've got you now. You're not going to get away

with that, you hear?" He raised the gun. Pat screamed.

Someone shouted. There was a shot, a spurt of fire, and the lamp in the room went out. They were plunged into darkness. Bewildered, the twins cowered in their corner. Who had shot out the light? Surely not the convict. He had just time to swear a mighty oath when the door burst open. There was noise and confusion, and the sound of scuffling masculine feet.

"Flash your light, Dick. Flash it. Over here," shouted Welton Duer.

A flashlight played quickly here and there, and lighted up the room in streaks. The convict shot in the direction of the light. But his shot went wild. He was rushed from behind, and with a crash, fell to the floor.

There was a sound of thrashing on the floor. "Get something to tie him up with."

Dick flashed his light on the bed, and grabbed up a sheet. He tore strips off it, and helped Duer to tie up the convict.

Yamoto, in the meanwhile, had found a new lamp, and had lighted it. He turned it up on a strange scene. On the floor lay the convict, trussed up clumsily in the sheet ropes. Above him, panting, stood Welton Duer, and next to him, Dick, looking for all the world like a tramp himself.

The door opened again and Mavis Martin came in. She rushed over to the twins. "Oh, you poor dears," she cried, and took them in her arms.

"Humph," said Welton Duer. "Poor dears. Look what the 'poor dears' got themselves and us into."

The twins looked contrite.

Mavis shook her head. "Don't scold them now," she said. "They've been through enough. Wait until they've had some rest, and have got over this."

And Welton Duer said no more that night.

It was Dick who made the arrangements to have their captive transported into town. "Yamoto," said Dick, "the reward is yours. You captured him."

"Oh, no, oh, no." Yamoto was grinning his broadest grin. "Patty and Jo catch him. Yamoto no catch nothing."

But he beamed at them all, and especially at Mr. Duer and Mavis Martin, and the wonderful silence that Mr. Duer maintained as soon as Mavis had spoken was astounding.

The strange party did not reach the Prentiss' house until the dawn was lighting the east. There they found the rest of the house party agog with excitement, and before they had told their story, the sun was high.

CHAPTER 12

Explanations

IT TOOK a few days for the twins to recover from their Christmas Eve experiences, but then they were as full of energy and the desire to be active as ever.

"But no getting into scrapes," warned Mavis Martin.

"And no detective work," warned Welton Duer.

The twins looked properly penitent. They felt then that they would never get into another scrape again. But whether they would or not was another question which we shall not go into now.

Welton Duer they found charming. He was all that a guardian should be, and they felt that he would make up to them for all the years that they had been friendless and alone. But there was Mavis—she and Welty had told the twins about their old romance, and how it had been renewed. Were they to lose Welty now as soon as they had found him? Pat and Jo, although they loved Mavis, looked upon her now with eyes of jealousy. Mavis had everything. Why must she have their

Welty, too? It didn't seem fair, somehow. But when they looked at Mavis and talked to her and were near her, then they could not feel jealous of such a radiant being, who deserved everything that she had.

The day before the twins were to leave for school, they planned a last skating party. Most of the other house guests had left the Prentiss', and Mavis, Duer, the twins and Dick were together the greater part of the time.

They had a jolly tea, the five of them, and then took their skates and went down to the lake, where the ice had been swept and smoothed into a glassy pond for skating.

It was a brisk day, and the men built a fire at the edge of the ice, and pulled up a long log for the girls to sit on.

Pat was the first on the ice. She glided gracefully out with long easy motions, and was soon far away from the group at the fire.

"Let's get her," cried Dick to Jo, and together they started after her, digging the points of their skates into the soft snow, and swinging out in a racing stride. They soon caught up to Pat, and the three of them skated out there, showing off, teaching each other fancy figures, and racing wildly from one point to another. Finally they raced back to the fire, and threw themselves wearily down in front of it.

"Whew," said Dick. "Those two wear me out. I'm going into secret training, and next time they come out here, I'll beat them hollow."

"Next time?" cried Pat. "We haven't been invited, you know."

Welton Duer laughed. He looked at Mavis, who looked back at him with shining eyes.

"Shall we tell them now, Mavis?"

The girl nodded her head. Her cheeks were flaming, not only with the cold, but with her emotion.

So Duer told them. "You see," he said rather hesitatingly, "well, you see, it's this way."

Mavis laughed. "I'd better tell, before we all freeze to death," she said.

The twins looked from one to the other. They felt that they could guess what was coming next.

"Welty and I are going to be married," said Mavis.

She looked with gleaming eyes at the twins. There was a little silence. Then Jo, who felt that something gay must be said, tried her best to say cheerfully, "Why, how lovely, Mavis, we're so pleased. And Welty."

But there was a little flat note in her tone.

Mavis went on:

"And we want to know if you two will live with us. We want you to, you know. You'll be our own children. Would you like that?"

Would they like that? Pat looked at Jo and Jo at Pat.

A home at last. Real parents! After all those years of being batted about. They flew to Mavis and embraced her.

"Oh, Mavis, darling. We'll love it. There's nothing we'd love better. If you'll only let us stay with you!"

Welton Duer, standing outside that loving group, broke in:

"Here, here, where do I come in? After all, you're going to live with me, too, you know. And I'm going to be the stern papa, and see that you don't get into trouble."

The twins turned shyly to him. They were still just a little afraid of their guardian, but he looked so lonesome and forlorn, so kind and wistful standing there that they, with one impulse, staggered awkwardly over on their skates and included him in their embrace.

Duer beamed. "And to think that at one time I was afraid of you."

The twins stared. "Afraid? What do you mean?" asked Pat.

"Afraid. That's what I mean. I was afraid to meet you two. You see, I'd been a bachelor so long, and was so sure that I didn't like women, that I became afraid of them. That's why I never came to see you, or had you here. Then when I finally felt so conscience-stricken that I had to invite you out here, I got cold feet at the last minute, and couldn't face you. That's the truth now, and it's out. I wouldn't even admit it to myself. I told myself that I didn't want to be bothered, and that I could work better out in the cabin, but I really didn't mean that. I was scared to death, that's all."

The twins laughed. "You were scared of us, and we were scared of you."

Then Pat said seriously, "But Welty, you needn't be afraid of us any longer."

The man looked down at her and laughed. "No, I'm not. I'm really not."

"And when we graduate, we can come right out here and live with you and Mavis?"

"That's it. Only we'll not live here all the time. There are lots of places we must go. There's all of America to see and, perhaps later, Europe, and Africa and Asia besides. Why, I don't know where we're going to find time to go all the places we're going."

Life seemed very pleasant at that moment. The wind had died down, and dusk was setting in fast. The only restless member of that happy little group was Dick, who skated around in little circles, looking forlorn.

Finally he skated over to the fire and said bluntly:

"And where do I come in? Here you've let me meet these two grand people, Welty, and you're talking about taking them away already."

Welty looked at him and laughed. "You come in whenever you care to, Dick. You'll always be the best friend the family ever had."

"I like that first rate," said Dick. "I think I'll be just that." He linked arms with Jo, and together they skated away. When they came back, they found that Yamoto had joined the group, bringing with him a huge hamper of food.

"Mm, steaks!" said Dick. "Bring on your grill. I'll cook them."

Soon the delicious aroma of roasting meat rose on the air. Whatever the emotions that any of them had experienced that afternoon, they were all equally hungry. Eagerly they awaited the food, while Yamoto unpacked the rest of the hamper.

"Well, Yamoto," said his master, "I suppose that you'll be taking all that reward money back to Japan. Surely you're not going to stay with us."

Yamoto grinned and went on with his work. "I stay here," he announced. "Yamoto must take care of evlybody. Mlissee Jo and Pat and Mavis."

"All of us?" laughed Mavis.

Yamoto nodded. "When you melly Mlister Dluer, Yamoto come be your servant."

"When I marry? Why, what makes you think I'm going to marry Mr. Duer?"

"Yamoto know." And that was that.

After they had eaten and put out their fire, the six of them walked back through the darkness over the scrunching snow to the Lodge. They talked very little, but as they neared the Lodge, Jo spoke.

"Do you know," she said. "I think that Pat and I are pretty good detectives."

"Why do you say that?" asked Welton Duer.

"Well, the test of a good detective is the fact that he finds things. And we've found things, Pat and I. We've been here just two weeks, and we've found what we wanted most in the world. We've found a home and people to love us. And that's good detectiving, if I must say so myself."

"It is, indeed," said Dick. "You ought to go in for that professionally."

Jo looked at him. "We might, at that. Now, what should we call ourselves. Oh, I know, Dick, you must paint us a sign right away."

"And what shall I paint on it?"

"Why, just 'Patty and Jo, Detectives.'"

CHAPTER 13

Back at Miss Langton's

PAT and Jo had the honor of giving the first tea when they got back to school. It was an informal affair, one of those teas that is not planned, but just happens. Their particular cronies had just naturally gathered at their regular meeting place, the twins' room, to talk over their Christmas adventures, exchange notes as to their Christmas presents, and generally get back into the swing of boarding-school gossip. Someone had suggested tea, the suggestion had seemed a good one, and the meeting turned into a tea.

"I'll bring down my new electric hot plate," suggested Meg Halliday. "My family was certainly sensible when it came to my Christmas presents. They gave me lounging pajamas, and the hot plate to cook on. My brother says that that's about all I need here at Miss Langton's. Little does he know how hard we have to work."

Hortie Horton laughed. "Your family knows you,

Meg. They couldn't have given you better presents. But really, they oughtn't to encourage your loafing that way."

"Meg needs no encouragement." This wicked remark came from Pat, who was vigorously performing her duties as hostess by cutting slices and slices of bread for toast.

"Who said that?" cried Meg.

Pat looked about innocently. "That was probably your conscience, my love," she laughed. "Now, you run and get your plate, and we'll forget that anybody said anything. Show us that you're really as ambitious as can be."

Meg's haste in leaving the room did indeed make her reputation for laziness seem unfair, but then, the sooner she brought the hot plate, the sooner would she have her tea. There was method to her hasty departure.

"Meg was certainly lucky in her Christmas presents, wasn't she?" said Liz Crane. "My family gave me a portable typewriter. Of course, that's a grand present. I've wanted one for years. But then, I think that it's a gentle hint for little Liz to get to work, don't you?"

"You don't need any encouragement in that line, Liz," Jo put in, from her favorite position in the window seat. "You do more work than any ten people around here. If you're not the valedictorian of our class this June, I don't know who will be."

"You," said Liz shortly.

Jo blushed. "Oh, not at all," she said quickly. "I won't even rate first honors."

By first honors she meant the most coveted honors given to the graduating girls at Miss Langton's. These were won by only a very few. The other honor students received either second or third honors. The rest of the class just trailed behind. Jo thought of how proud she would be if she could walk to the platform with the small group of first honor girls. But the pride would be tempered, in fact it would be non-existent, if Pat could not walk with her. Pat was an excellent student, except in mathematics. Her imaginative mind could not be trained to work in the steady grooves demanded by mathematics. On the other hand, Jo herself was the star of the mathematics class, but her English, well, in English composition, Pat could walk circles all around her. She made up her mind that she was going to start immediately to tutor Pat through the last term of math, and have Pat likewise tutor her through English, so that the two of them would graduate with honors, if not first, then second.

Her reverie was broken by the return of Meg with the hot plate.

"Are you people talking about work yet?" she called out. "Jo Faraday, I never saw anybody like you. There you lie doing nothing at all and talking about work as though you meant it."

"Ho, hum," sighed Jo, untangling herself and sitting up. "I don't see anything for me to do in this ambitious group. All I can do is drink your tea when it's finished."

"Thanks," said Meg.

"Thanks are in order," said Jo. "I've drunk your tea before."

"I ignore you," said Meg, and busied herself with the tea kettle.

Jo got up to get out the tea things and set them on the card table which served as a tea table. It was an ivory china set decorated with a rim of tiny flowers, which Mrs. Prentiss had given them as a parting gift. They were from her own collection of dishes, and the twins appreciated the value of such a gift, and the love that went with it. "You can't ignore me long," said Jo, as she carefully set down the cups and saucers, "or you'll have to drink your tea out of a tin basin. Only our very special friends can drink out of these cups."

The girls all gathered around to look at and admire the china. "Christmas presents?"

"Yes," answered Pat. "And handle with care. They're precious."

"They're beautiful," said Hortie. "You two twins have been as secret as anything about your Christmas. Whatever did happen? Aren't you going to tell us?"

Pat and Jo exchanged glances. "Shall we tell them?" grinned Jo.

"Of course," said Pat. "You know, we wanted to work up a good deal of suspense. We've intended all along to tell you what happened."

"Leave it to the twins to have a rip-roaring time," said Meg. "Any place Pat and Jo chance to be becomes just a welter of excitement. They have all the luck. I do believe that if I were in the midst of a war it would be a very unexciting war. But Pat and Jo can go up to the woods, miles from civilization, and have so many adventures they can't tell them all."

She was interrupted by the singing of the tea kettle.

"Let's have our tea," said Pat, "before Meg breaks down."

"Meg's right, though," said Hortie. "You two are the greatest pair for having adventures. Tell us about them, or we'll burst."

"Oh, don't burst," said Jo. "At least, not before you've had your tea, Hortie. We can't begin any story until we've had that."

They had their tea, then, consuming quantities of toast and strong sweet tea, and talking about the coming semester, which was to be their last. Then the girls all cleared the table, and Pat and Liz took the dishes down the hall to wash them in the little kitchen provided for these impromptu lunches. When they got back, they found the other three reclining in various positions of ease about the room.

"Come on," called Hortie. "We're ready for the story. THE GREAT ADVENTURE, or THE FARADAY TWINS AT HARKER'S COVE. It had better be exciting, too. We're expecting a lot."

"Oh, it will be exciting, all right," said Jo. "But first, to put you into the mood, I'm going to show you one of our Christmas presents."

She went over to her trunk, and took a box out of one of the drawers. Out of the box she took a small tissue-wrapped object. She handed it to Meg. "Open it," she said.

Meg undid the package. She gave a little scream. "What is it?" she cried, hastily pushing the package aside. Liz picked it up, and put it down just as quickly. She looked in horror at Jo, and then at Pat, who were watching their friends with quiet amusement. Hortie, her curiosity aroused, went over to the package. She did not touch it, but poked it about until she could see the contents. When she had, she was glad that she had not touched it.

"What on earth is it?" she asked in her turn.

"Oh, a head," said Jo, casually.

The three girls screamed again. "A head?"

"Yes." It was Pat who spoke this time. "It's a human head, shrunken to that size. The headhunters did that to their victims, you know. It was a dear possession of our guardian's, but he gave it to us for Christmas."

Meg shuddered. "Oh, dear, I don't think I'd like to have it around. It gives me the creeps just to look at it. Please take it away, Jo."

Jo tenderly picked up the mummified head and put it back in its box. "We've grown rather fond of it," she said. "You do get used to it, you know. We didn't like it any more than you do when we first saw it. In fact, I think it affected us the same way."

"That's why we wanted to show it to you," went on Pat. "We wanted to get you into the mood of our story. Alonzo was the first to greet us up at the Lodge."

"Alonzo?"

"Oh, yes, we call him Alonzo. Well, now that you are all ready for the story, we can begin. Do you want to tell it, Jo?"

"Not at all," said Jo. "If it's going to be a good story, you've got to tell it, Pat."

Pat consented readily enough. Having an adventure is exciting enough, but retelling it, still more exciting. So she told her friends the tale of their adventures at Welton Duer's lodge. When she finished, there was a silence. Then Liz spoke:

"Do you mean to tell me that all those things happened to you in two weeks?"

Pat nodded. Then Liz said, "What a wonderful story that would make." She gazed at the twins raptly for a few moments and then suddenly jumped up. "I've got an idea!" she cried. "You people wait here. I'll be back in a moment." She dashed out of the room. The four girls looked at one another in astonishment. What on earth had happened to the usually staid Liz? The girl solved the problem for them, however, by reappearing in a short time, jubilantly waving a magazine in her hand.

"Just the thing!" she panted, as she thrust the magazine into Pat's hand. "Here, read that!"

"Read what?"

"Page 26," answered the girl. "There's a contest being held for high-school and college people; a short-story contest. There are several divisions—and one's for an adventure story. I was going to try something myself —not the adventure story, of course; one of the essays or something. But if you two don't write out your story and send it in, I'm going to disown you. Now, how about it?"

Jo and Pat rapidly read the rules of the contest in the magazine. It was exactly as Liz had said. A prize of five hundred dollars was being offered in the adventure-story division of the contest, for the best true adventure written by a high-school student.

"Oh, but we haven't a chance," said Jo. "There will be entries from all over the country. The cleverest people will send in stories—people who can really write."

Liz shook her by the shoulder. "Silly," she chided. "Don't you know that you don't have to be a grand writer to write up that adventure of yours? Just tell it as you've told it today, and I think that you'll win hands down."

Jo turned to Pat. "Of course, Pat will have to do the writing. It sounds like a lot of fun to me. Even if we don't win anything, it will be good for us to get our story written out. What do you say, Pat?"

Pat's eyes were shining with excitement. "I think it will be grand. We'll collaborate, darling. It'll be good for both of us. It will stir your sluggish little imagination," she added with a laugh, "and it will pin me down to details, and make me more accurate. How about it?"

Liz was pleased and proud. "With the Faraday brains, and the Faraday luck, it's going to be a sure thing. You can use my new portable for typing your manuscript, and I'll help you go over the thing for mistakes."

"You're a peach," said Jo. "I don't see how the combination could be beat, Pat and you and I."

For days and days the twins hung out the "Do Not Disturb" sign on their door. For nights and nights the tip tap tap of their typewriter could be heard breaking the stillness of the corridors.

At last it was finished, and the twins, a little wan and worn, again showed themselves at the parties and gatherings of their friends.

The month before graduation was not a happy one for the twins. They were faced with the situation of having no one present at their graduation, that is, no one who was near and dear to them. The guest rooms at Miss Langton's were full to overflowing with parents of girls, all of whom had come for the festivities that preceded graduation. But none of the rooms held any Faradays.

Welton Duer had written to them just two weeks before. He had been called to the west coast on business, and he and Mavis had taken the opportunity to get married and make this their honeymoon trip. He doubted whether he would be able to reach the east before their graduation. However, they were to stay at Miss Langton's until he and Mavis came for them. That was little consolation. What good had it done them to find lovely relatives if they were going to be on the west coast at a time when they needed them? What fun would they get out of graduation when all the other girls were proudly taking their parents about to teas and parties, and they had nobody but themselves? Of course, the parents of their friends adopted them temporarily, but they could not make up for real relatives.

Jo was gloomily meditating upon this state of affairs when Pat burst frantically into the room. "Jo, darling! I've just been down to the postoffice to get the school mail. There were only two letters," she panted.

"Well?" said Jo, "what is so exciting about that?" She would not be stirred out of her melancholy mood.

"But they're both for us! Look, Jo, look. I could hardly wait to get back here. One's from Dick, and the other's from New York. From the publisher of the magazine we sent our story to! Jo, I almost tore open the letter on the way home here, but I controlled myself."

Jo jumped to her feet. Gone was all apathy. She grasped one end of the paper, and together they read it. "Pay to the order of Josephine and Patricia Faraday, the sum of . . . . . $500.00."

"The first prize! Whoopee!"

"Oh, let's go tell everybody. They'll be delighted," crowed Pat. "Golly, Jo, this makes up for everything, even Welty's not being here."

Jo had subsided by this time, and sank into a chair. "Wait a minute," she said, "before you tell anybody else." Then after a pause broken by her sister's exuberant question as to why they shouldn't tell everybody their good fortune, she said, "There wasn't any mail for anybody else, was there?"

"Why, no," said Pat. "Only the two for us."

"Then," said Jo, "Liz didn't win a prize with her essay."

Pat's face fell. "I never thought of that," she said soberly. "I was so glad about ours that I didn't think of poor Liz."

The two sat in silence a while. Then Pat said: "And she needs the money so much more than we do. But really, Jo, I don't see what we can do. She certainly wouldn't take the money if we offered it to her."

"Oh, no," said Jo, almost in horror. "You know she wouldn't do that. I wouldn't think of asking her to take it." Jo was tearing open the other letter, which was addressed to her. She cast her eye down the dashingly written page, brightening perceptibly as she read on.

"Dick's coming!" she announced triumphantly.

"He is! When?" Pat perked up immediately. "How in the world—"

"He's finished with his examinations early," went on Jo. "His mother is visiting some friends in the east, and he and Jack Halley, his roommate, are going to call for her, and drive her up to Wisconsin. They're going to stop here on their way."

"When do they get here?"

"He says on the 28th. That's tomorrow! Oh, hooray! Won't that be wonderful, having Dick and his mother. It's almost as good as having Welty and Mavis."

"Almost," said Pat. "We'll have to let Miss Langton know. The boys will probably stay down in the village, but Mrs. Prentiss can have a guest room here if there's one left."

So busy were the girls in planning for their guests that they almost forgot the important problem of their prize money, until Jo said suddenly:

"I've an idea about our contest prize. Listen." And

she unfolded a plan to Pat that thoroughly met with that girl's approval.

"Oh, great. Jo, you would get a bright idea like that."

"It's nothing," said Jo lightly. "Just a remarkable mind, that's all." Then she became serious. "But the most important thing for us to do now is to keep quiet about winning the contest. Nobody will know about it until next month, if we don't tell them. But if it leaks out our plan is ruined."

Pat looked downcast. "It's going to be hard," she said.

But it wasn't as hard as she thought, keeping the secret of their success in the contest. They were so busy dashing madly about getting ready for graduation, and entertaining Dick and Mrs. Prentiss and Jack Halley that they did not have time to think about their prize, much less talk about it. That is, to anybody except one person.

The twins spent a great deal of time closeted with Mrs. Prentiss, until Dick and Jack pretended to grow jealous.

"Don't we get in on these secrets?" asked Dick, glowering at Jo.

Jo shook her head. "You wouldn't understand," she said haughtily, "being a man."

"We're good for something, we men," said Jack Halley. "How about taking a row on the lake? At least we can row."

Graduation day dawned bright and clear and warm.

Nothing was lacking. That is, nothing lacking except to the twins. They would have loved to feel that Welton Duer and Mavis were in the audience watching them walk demurely down the path to the flower-banked terrace where the graduating class was to sit.

The ceremonies were simple and soon over, and Miss Langton advanced to the front of the stage. There was a ripple through the audience, and among the girls on the platform, for it was the moment when prizes were to be awarded.

Miss Langton was speaking. "It is with pleasure that I therefore award first honors in scholarship to Miss Elizabeth Crane. It gives me added pleasure to announce that this year there is a money award to go to the girl achieving this highest standing in scholarship. I therefore award first honors in scholarship to Miss Paul Prentiss, the donor, a prize of five hundred dollars."

There was a burst of applause that lasted for a full minute. The girls on the platform buzzed with excitement, all trying to congratulate Liz at once. Pat and Jo did not look at each other. Their plan had worked. Mrs. Prentiss had proved a good sport, and let the money be given in her name. Liz would never know that it had been the prize money. And there was nothing that the girls would rather have done with it.

Miss Langton announced the names of the honors winners. Pat and Jo gained second honors in scholarship; first in athletics. The announcements seemed over. But Miss Langton still stood in her place.

"There is one last award to be made," she said. "This also is a new award, never offered before. The donor is anonymous, and has offered the sum of five hundred dollars to be given to the girl who has done the most for her class. It is called the Service Prize. In this case we had great difficulty in making the decision as to who should receive this money."

There was a great buzzing and stirring in the audience and among the girls.

"We have finally decided," said Miss Langton, "to divide the prize, and award one-half to Miss Patricia Faraday, and one-half to Miss Josephine Faraday."

There was a spontaneous cheer from the platform, and hearty applause from the audience, and Jo and Pat, even in their astonishment and surprise, could hear Dick Prentiss above everybody else.

The ceremonies were over. The girls filed down from the platform, to receive the congratulations and good wishes of their proud friends and relatives in the audience. Pat and Jo had a hard time finding the Prentisses, since they were stopped and congratulated on all sides by their chums. But finally they came to the edge of the group, where Jo saw Mrs. Prentiss and Dick talking to some strangers.

But were they strangers? Oh, not that tall slim figure and the short slim one beside him! It was Welty and

BACK AT MISS LANGTON'S

Mavis! The girls broke into a run, and flung themselves into their arms.

There were many things to be said, many questions to be asked. But Welty answered them all in good time. He and Mavis had flown east, in order to arrive at the twins' graduation. "And mighty glad we did," said Welton Duer. "I wouldn't have liked to miss the announcement making you two millionaires."

"Oh, not quite," said Jo, her eyes shining. "But who do you suppose the anonymous donor can be?"

Mrs. Prentiss smiled. Dick smiled, too. "Well, you twins, that oughtn't to be hard to solve. Not for two such clever girls as Pat and Jo, Detectives."

FALCON  BOOKS

For Girls

Champion's Choice BY JOHN R. TUNIS
Patty and Jo, Detectives BY ELSIE WRIGHT
Patty and Jo, The Case of the Toy Drummer BY JANET
    KNOX

BY KAY LYTTLETON

Jean Craig Grows Up
Jean Craig in New York
Jean Craig Finds Romance
Jean Craig, Nurse
Jean Craig, Graduate Nurse

BY JEAN MCKECHNIE

Penny Allen and the Mystery of the Haunted House
Penny Allen and the Mystery of the Hidden Treasure

For Boys

The Spirit of the Border BY ZANE GREY
The Last Trail BY ZANE GREY
Call to Adventure BY ROBERT SPIERS BENJAMIN
Champs on Ice BY JACK WRIGHT
On the Forty-Yard Line BY JACK WRIGHT
The Strike-Out King BY JULIAN DE VRIES
The Winning Basket BY DUANE YARNELL
Over the Hurdles BY EMMETT MAUM
Boys' Book of Famous Soldiers BY J. WALKER MCSPADDEN
Boys' Book of Famous Fliers BY CAPT. J. J. GRAYSON
Boys' Book of Sea Battles BY CHELSEA CURTIS FRASER
Through Forest and Stream BY DUANE YARNELL

BY CAPWELL WYCKOFF

The Mercer Boys' Cruise on the Lassie
The Mercer Boys at Woodcrest
The Mercer Boys on a Treasure Hunt
The Mercer Boys' Mystery Case
The Mercer Boys with the Coast Guard
The Mercer Boys in the Ghost Patrol